I0453793

URBAN WOLF

Urban Wolf
An anthology with stories by Linda Thomas-Sundstrom
and Jillian Stone

Wolf in the City Copyright © 2017 Linda Thomas-Sundstrom
Wolf, Interrupted Copyright © 2017 Jillian Stone

Published by GothicScapes™
Cover art: Jillian Stone

All rights reserved. No part of this publication may be reproduced, stored in or introduced into a retrieval system, or transmitted in any form, or by any means (electronic, mechanical, photocopying, recording, or otherwise) without prior written permission of both the copyright owner and the above publisher of this book.

This is a work of fiction. Names, characters, places, brands, and incidents are either the product of the author's imagination or are used fictitiously. The author acknowledges the trademarked status and trademark owners of various products referenced in this work of fiction which have been used without permission. The publication of use of these trademarks is not authorized, associated with, or sponsored by the trademark owners.

ISBN: 978-0-9858714-8-2

URBAN WOLF

ANTHOLOGY

includes

WOLF IN THE CITY

and

WOLF, INTERRUPTED

Wolf in the City

Linda Thomas-Sundstrom

Chapter

ONE

Jared James didn't want to prowl the streets. He wasn't particularly fond of nighttime hours after having encountered the meaning of true darkness a year ago. Paying for that horror-filled night in L.A. meant he'd forever be in debt.

But that was then.

This was now.

And hindsight was a bitch.

He stood on a lonely street corner in a less popular area of Los Angeles that was free of cars at this late hour. It was close to midnight. Good folks were either asleep or safe in their homes. They certainly weren't strolling in an area that most cops and gangbangers avoided after dark.

Not that he was completely alone though. Preternaturally super-charged senses told him there was something else hanging around. Already, his bones were pulsing with that knowledge, the way they always did when trouble was a foregone conclusion.

"I know you're here," he muttered without glancing up at the narrow slit of sky visible between the buildings, aiming his comment at the unseen presence hovering nearby. That presence had become like a pressure in his mind. One he didn't recognize.

The moon wasn't visible from where he stood. Without that moon's particular brand of celestial voodoo, he looked like every other human being on the planet. To any onlooker stupid enough to be around, he'd appear to be just another idiot who had ventured too far from nearby safe zones.

As long as he remained in the shadows, out of the moonlight, the moon had to wait her turn for demanding his full attention, which was a good thing since right that minute other issues were more worrisome. Like the strangely elusive presence nipping at his awareness with an unshakable premonition of danger.

Rolling his shoulders was a habitual move meant to ease his tension that never actually worked. Jared tilted his head to listen for sounds, knowing in his bones that it was going to be that kind of night. No calm. No peace. Problems piling up. Besides that lurking, unseen, pestering presence hovering in the shadows, and against all levels of common sense, there were people heading his way. Imbeciles ignoring the potential hazards of the area.

This wasn't just bad news, it could prove to be lethal for those humans if the other presence he detected in the shadows had the word *evil* stamped on its forehead. If a dangerous anomaly chose this particular time to show itself in order to prey on the humans, tonight could turn out to be one of L.A.'s little midnight battlefields, pitting humans against darker things with a hunger for fragile mortal souls.

Hell, he had been a victim of a battle like that.

No other reason could have brought him here now, other than the fact that somebody had to keep watch for predators. And as fate would have it, he had more or less volunteered for the job.

Jared tried the shoulder-easing routine again to no avail. Friction was building in the atmosphere and everything about tonight rubbed him the wrong way. He had to get the humans out of here before the other thing in the shadows showed up.

Attuned to a set of new sounds, Jared's heart rate revved. *Stupid mortals,* he wanted to shout, because who in their right mind would come anywhere near this street tonight, except for misfits with a death wish?

He scuffed the toe of his boot against the pavement where a puddle of moonlight had pooled. For him, moonlight was a whole other issue in need of careful monitoring. Forgetting about that light would be a mistake. Later though, and if his premonition came true about the danger, that light might come in handy if push came to shove with the invisible entity practically breathing down his neck.

In werewolf form, he was more than twice as strong as any man. All he had to do to access his wolf was to step into that light.

It was strange how he had begun to define people as both humans and mortals without including himself. He was now a thing apart. The term *human* had ceased to cover what he had become. *Creature* was a better choice, and he had the claws to prove it. He was a *werewolf* –half man, half beast—and had been since hell had come calling on a night like this one. That night was something he didn't talk about.

Couldn't talk about. Who would believe him if he tried?

Lessons learned after his life-changing event had been hard won, such as learning to be overly careful when a full moon rode the skies. Early on, and on more than one occasion, he had almost succeeded in accidentally letting the world in on the secret about other two-legged species' sharing their space.

The aftermath of a slip-up like that would have been a severe wakeup call for Joe Public. Humans would have found out about werewolves, and he would have been responsible for outing that particular secret.

He preferred to search for the source of his malady to make sure what happened to him didn't happen to anyone else, at least in the part of the city so near to his home. Of course, he hadn't yet found the monster that had passed along the nasty wolf virus to him, if in fact a virus is what made a man a werewolf. He had never met another werewolf face-to-face, and therefore had no basis for determining exactly what had happened to him. Still, since he was a werewolf, there had to be others. What were the odds that the monster he had encountered out here had never made another beast?

Thing was… since becoming *other,* Jared figured there had to be more kinds of creatures sharing that description. Case in point, the as-yet unknown entity hiding in the shadows. He just wasn't sure what those other creatures might turn out to be.

"I get it. You're close," he whispered to the lurker. "Let's keep it that way, okay?"

Caution flags were waving. Care was needed here. Above all, Jared had to be mindful of the rules governing his condition. After a tough first year, those instincts were nearly second-nature to him now, though every once in a while he might have preferred to forget what he had become.

Silence filled the shadows at his back.

If the elusive creature crowding his position on the corner tonight had heard his comment, it didn't verbally respond. Yet more needling sensations on the back of Jared's neck brought on a chill, as though the other creature had sent back a silent message he couldn't quite grasp.

Clearly, he had to find out what that elusive sucker was and whether it had plans for the humans heading their way. As an ex-cop and the area's self-appointed guardian, it was his job to keep the place safe.

That's what Jared told himself, anyway. *Keep the place safe.* The real reason for hanging out here was his intrinsic need to find the abomination that had savaged him and made him into something other than his former self. He wanted to put that monster out of its misery.

"Humans, what are you thinking?" he said out loud, ditching the inward self-analysis. Images of the people heading his way became clearer now. There were two. Males. Their scent drifted to him on an almost non-existent breeze, polluting the night.

Wait. Watch. Keep to the shadows, Jared reminded himself without announcing his presence. If those men passed by where he stood, things would be fine. If something else stepped out of the shadows to accost these guys, he'd see some action.

Usually, shadows were his friends. Tonight, he didn't like sharing the dark, but it seemed like he had no choice in the matter.

Patience.

Wait...

Stillness was uncomfortable for him. His metabolism ran hot. Sometimes he had an urge to run and howl like his ancient ancestors, but as a detective on personal leave from the LAPD, that kind of nonsense would called in the troops.

It was imperative for him to keep his mind intact, alert, and remain the master of his more familiar shape. The one small piece of his soul left to him is what made him concerned for others still ignorant of the kind of damage a set of sharp claws and canines could inflict on an unsuspecting human being. If he lost that kind of insight, he'd be sunk.

The two humans were getting closer. Taking their time.

Good thing for them—a goddamn lucky break, actually—was the fact that Jared James was on full alert.

The sound of shoes slapping the sidewalk prevented Jared from turning to look behind him. He uttered a silent curse aimed at the as-yet invisible entity in the shadows.

Who are you?

Why are you bugging me?

Was that creature watching him? Gauging his intent?

Could that creature tell that Jared James's molecules had been rearranged on a dark fall night like this one, detouring his system from normal to abstract?

The shadowy presence he detected behind him wasn't a werewolf. Jared was fairly sure he would have known if it were. So, what other kind of monster did that leave?

He was pretty sure he was about to find out.

Fisting his hands, he took a tentative step forward, moving to the head of the alley. The people with the loud footsteps stank of cigarettes and cheap hair gel. Giving off odors like that would make them fair game and easy pickings for any predator trolling the area.

Jared waited for them, anxious, wary, melding with the dark spaces between the two tall buildings. His black leather jacket would be his only means of camouflage if the two males looked at him. What the coat couldn't do was ward off moonlight. Nothing short of hiding from the light forever would have been good for that.

The males turned a corner twenty feet from where Jared leaned against an old brick wall covered with graffiti. More messages about these guys came to him via the night's cool, transparent airwaves.

One of them wore aftershave. One wore a wristwatch that ticked away the hours, minutes, seconds of what could perhaps be their last few seconds on Earth if Jared's instincts were right and the night proved to be unlucky.

That other nuisance, the one he couldn't yet

pinpoint but that continually set off on his internal warning system for anomalies, also continued to press closer. Jared had no idea what to expect.

Vigilance was the key here.

Patience...

The two men finally closed the distance. From a few paces away, Jared heard laughter. Either they were unconcerned about where they were, or they truly were ignorant of things that merely posed for human on street corners.

Five feet away now.

Three.

A glint of metal flashed from one guy's hand. Maybe they carried weapons to defend themselves, which in some instances could have been prudent.

When their footsteps abruptly ceased, two arch human gazes locked onto Jared in a predatory way that should have made anyone's skin crawl. Jared James wasn't just an ordinary person, though. *Really,* he wanted to tell these guys, *I'm not a person at all.*

Their motives were obvious. These humans weren't out for a pleasurable stroll or trying to get somewhere. Nor were they merely planning to defend themselves by wielding a weapon. These guys were assuming the role of aggressors and looking for someone to hurt. The flash of excitement in their eyes gave them away.

The taller of the two had a tight grip on the hilt of a knife, probably because a gun would have made too much noise. Face contorted with malicious intent, that guy lunged toward Jared with his lips curled into a sneer.

Utilizing lightning-fast reflexes, Jared let them know he was not going to be a victim here. Reaching out, he caught hold of the blade that had been meant to do him damage and wrenched it from the hand that had held it, withstanding the sting of the blade's sharp edge slicing through his palm.

"Give it up, freak," the guy shouted, producing a second blade.

Jared got the picture. These young hoodlums, who couldn't have been older than twenty-three or four, were out to score some valuables, and were about to become their own worst enemies. However, "giving it up"—which in this instance meant the possible forfeiture of Jared's life, since he didn't possess any valuables—also meant that there would be no one to protect these streets if he were to be harmed.

These were monsters, just not the kind of monsters he had initially intended to protect people from. Human savages like these two bastards wouldn't have cared who they accosted. These days, too many young people were out to get something without having to work for it.

"Not going to happen," Jared warned, his voice a deep rumble as he stepped toward the guy with the blade. "And I'm fully prepared for surprises."

Spinning in place so quickly the bastards barely had time to blink, Jared threw both guys into a state of momentary confusion when he didn't try to get away. That fraction of a second, while their mouths were agape, was all the time Jared needed to gain the upper hand.

In another wicked display of speed, he took the second knife away. With a bloody grip on both collars, he shoved the pair into the alley behind him, out of range of any possible passing cop cars and the iridescent spread of treacherous moonlight.

Pinning them to the wall with hardly any effort at all, Jared spoke with his face close to theirs. "Boys, it looks like you've picked the wrong victim tonight."

When he loosened his hold so they could speak, one of the men slid downward, toppling his partner. On their sorry asses, sitting on the gritty asphalt, these twenty-somethings didn't look half as arrogant or cocky as they had moments ago. They were bloodless and scared.

Jared's next growled remark rumbled like an earthquake rolling through town. "Now what shall we do with you, I wonder?"

Their faces could not have paled further. Neither of these guys made an attempt to answer his question.

"Maybe a warning will suffice on this one occasion? If you were to get off fairly easily just this once, I'd assume you might think twice about doing this kind of thing again. Because if you were to see me a second time, there'd better be an army along to back you up."

Another cool tingle at the nape of his neck competed for Jared's attention. He glanced up to make sure the moon wasn't about to do something that would enlighten these two stunned bastards about the world of werewolves… although that would have served these guys right.

"Get your asses up and going before I forget

about feeling charitable," he said.

Standing took time. Once they were on their feet, Jared backed slowly out of the alley, careful to keep close to the wall. With the two knives safely in his pocket, he turned back toward the corner of the alley that had become his outlook post.

But he was stopped by another icy wave of chills before he had gone ten feet. It wasn't the moon doing this. He was sure about that. From somewhere close, and over his head, a low-pitched female voice called out to him with a cynical tone.

"Really? They'd need an army?"

C h a p t e r

TWO

There was movement to his right, above him. Hands raised, ready to fight, Jared spun around to locate the speaker. That wasn't so simple though, since the visitor had no heat signature, and his new Wereness located others by way of their body heat.

Muscles taut, senses focused, Jared strained to see into the shadows. "Figure of speech," he said.

The watcher he had detected early on appeared on the stone ledge above him, offering Jared another surprise. The female entity was human-like in shape, and almost could have passed for human. But wasn't.

She was tall, her silhouette extremely narrow. And she had been flexible enough to swing herself up to that ledge. Dressed in body-hugging clothes dark enough to blend with the night, Jared's unwelcome visitor gave off no viable scent for him to plug into his mental databanks.

Definitely not human. But what?

What kind of anomaly had no scent or heat signature?

What other type of being appeared to be human, but wasn't?

The night, Jared decided, had just gotten a whole

18

hell of a lot more interesting.

With the shadows at her back and a hood covering her hair, the female's face wasn't visible. The part about failing to notice how close she had actually been to his position on the corner gave Jared a twinge of dissatisfaction. This watcher could have had the upper hand if she'd wanted to, for the five seconds it would have taken before the brutality of Jared's full strength kicked in... and if she had been three feet taller, a hell of a lot broader, and also carried a machine gun.

Though she was drenched in shadows, Jared saw her raise one hand. The object she displayed glittered wickedly in a slender shaft of moonlight, garnering Jared's full attention. Across her palm lay one of the knives he had taken from the pair of ruffians he'd left humiliated in the alley. The same damn weapon they had waved at him.

Jared shoved a hand into his pocket.

Both knives were missing.

Growls of anger bubbled up inside him.

"Perhaps you've dropped something?" the cheeky female asked in a tone that somewhat resembled Jared's human growl.

Jared planted his feet in case his visitor opted for using the blade. "How did you manage to get that from my pocket?"

"I stole it." She balanced the knife on her palm as if testing its weight. "Using pure unadulterated talent, plus a little slight-of-hand."

After closing her fingers over the knife, she added, "There's blood on the blade."

Jared said noncommittally, "Seems so."

Traces of red stained the edge of the knife. Jared curled his fingers over his injured palm.

"The blood is yours," she said.

Since she had been watching him all along, Jared figured she already knew that without him having to confirm it.

"Why did you let those men go?" she asked.

"I don't hurt people if given a choice."

"Even when they want to hurt you?"

"Even then."

The wound on his hand was of no consequence. By tomorrow it would be fully healed, leaving only a thin white scar. Being a werewolf had that much going for it at least. His powers for healing were nothing short of miraculous. Right now though, as Jared squeezed his fist, several blood drops pattered onto the asphalt.

"You should get that tended to," the mysterious female suggested with her attention riveted to him.

"Thanks for your concern."

"I could fix it for you," she offered.

Jared eyed the creature even more warily. "The wound will heal."

"Yes, but my way might be more fun," she said.

Conversation between them was terse, yet interesting in a taunting, subversive way. Why wasn't the willowy thief with no heat signature running away from a big guy on a dark street? How far removed from term *civilized* was she going to turn out to be?

He had never met anyone like her, and by observing the way she watched the blood drip from his fist, Jared was fairly sure he finally had her pegged. His reaction to the idea was internal—a minor shakeup that spiraled through his system like a storm. He had never come across one of *them* before. In truth, he hadn't truly believed her species existed.

But her chest was quiet. No rapid heartbeat sounds. No pounding pulse. When she wasn't speaking, there was no intake or release of breath. It was obvious to Jared this stranger didn't fear the night or what might hide in it. Nor did she appear to be the least bit afraid of him.

Because she was a monster herself.

Jared searched her outline, noting every detail, hoping to prove to himself that the entity he was talking to wasn't merely a hallucination, and that fiction novels had actually gotten the existence of more than one species right.

The female on that ledge was a vampire.

"I'm as real as you are." She said this as if she had read his mind. "I guarantee you didn't conjure me."

Jared hated how his pulse moved upward a notch or two, and he again wondered about how long she had been observing him. If this little vampire could appear on his sensitive radar as nothing more than a ripple on the back of his neck, how many others of her kind could pull off that same kind of invisibility trick? How many like her were around that very minute?

He didn't turn around to look.

"I'm alone, in case you're wondering. For the moment, anyway," she said, reading him as easily as if he had posed his question aloud. But the fact that she was alone was good news if she was telling the truth.

A pale, languid hand gestured toward something in the distance. "Those two creeps you messed with back there are pissed off, on their feet again, and not at all happy with your performance."

"Performance?" Jared echoed.

She nodded. "You know. The fierce growl and blurry show of superhuman strength routine."

"Good thing you have their knives, then," Jared said.

"Yes. I suppose it is."

"Both knives, I presume?"

"Afraid so," she confirmed.

Jared couldn't find anything to say about that.

"Those hoodlums will know better than to try another attack on anyone here tonight for a ring or a watch," he said.

"And perhaps they misjudged your strength and won't be threatened by it or your act of leniency."

"Maybe they were scared straight," Jared said.

"Did you stop to consider that they might have been searching for you or some other type of being out here, with no particular interest in an actual robbery?" she suggested.

"What other type of beings are we talking about?"

He really wanted to see this mysterious female's face, and fought the impulse to jump up to the ledge. Would her appearance be similar to the way movies presented vampires—white-skinned and pasty, with red-rimmed eyes and protruding fangs? Maybe this little alley chat was a weird kind of vampire foreplay and the equivalent of a vamp's dinner bell.

"Possibly those guys are after my kind," she said, stopping any move toward her Jared might have thought to make by pointing at him, then at the ground where he stood. All that was missing from her gesture was a command for him to "*stay.*"

Still, she inched forward as though she had interpreted his thoughts about wanting to see her more clearly and would oblige his request to some small degree.

"Why would they be after you?" Jared asked. "Does anyone on this planet actually believe you exist?"

Thin shoulders shrugged. "A few people are in the know. Just like the few who know about you."

"You believe some people do?"

"Know about you? Oh yes. You can be sure of it," she replied.

Jared wasn't sure he liked that news. Nevertheless, he had to add *intelligent* to the list of considerations regarding this female. There was nothing wrong with the quickness of the vampire's wit, and no immediate evidence of a dead person's missing brain cells. She was sharp, quick, and seemed to know more about werewolves than he did.

"So, you're facing a werewolf, but worried about those guys in the alley?" he asked.

"I'm not worried about either of those things."

"You have their knives. Can we assume you know how to use them?" Jared pressed.

"Do you think I need knives for protection?"

The way her tone was anchored in cynicism made Jared believe that knives would have been absurd as a vampire's sole means of self-defense. He sorted through what little information he could recall about vampires without liking one single thing. They were supposed to be fast and dangerous. They were supposed to be lethal to anyone unfortunate enough to meet one. Already having lost their lives, vampires were aggressive because they didn't have much more to lose.

And vampires were reanimated dead people, which meant this female wasn't actually alive. Someone had, at one time or another, killed her. With his own traumatic journey from man to werewolf still strong within his memories, Jared felt a wave of sympathy for the vampire on that ledge, and for what she might have been through in order to become a vampire.

She leaned forward with her weight on her toes. Her thick-heeled black boots could have used a swipe with a clean rag and would no doubt cause some damage in a kick. Possibly her size was no indication of the kind of strengths she possessed.

Jared wasn't particularly keen to find that out.

"Aren't you going to lecture me on the pitfalls of being out here alone, without an escort?" she asked in a honeyed tone that didn't suit her. "You aren't going to tell me this area is no place for a lady?"

Jared shook his head. "If you can pilfer those knives from my pocket without me knowing it, I'll bet you have other talents that might render sentiments like that unnecessary. Am I right?"

"Infinitely right."

"Your speed might match mine?"

"Or be better," she said.

Jared went on. "So you do not, in fact, need weapons of any kind to protect yourself, due to the possession of talents other than slight-of-hand tricks?"

He didn't mention anything about fangs.

"Count on it," she agreed.

Jared continued to study this intriguing anomaly. "And I take it you're no lady in the strictest sense of the word."

"The human sense, you mean."

"Yes. That's what I mean."

"Pretty far from it," she said.

Half in and half out of the moonlight, the silver blade in her hand looked blue. The dim glow of a distant streetlight threw more shadows all around, keeping her face hidden from him. Jared's need to see her was growing. Cursing the shadows that kept him from discovering what a vampire's features would look like, his attention spiked when she raised her face to the thin stream of moonlight raining down, and her features began to fill in.

Jared withheld a note of surprise.

The first thing that stood out was the whiteness of her skin. Truth and fiction about her species merged in a colorlessness that made her flesh almost transparent.

She had sharp features on the gaunt side and dark eyes that seemed to look right through him.

Heavy-handed black makeup lined those eyes and also outlined her lips. Dark crescents, perfect half-moons, underscored her eyes as if she'd been either sleepless or ill before she had died.

The word *died* echoed in Jared's mind, because this vampire had been pretty once, and still was in a slightly scary way. A black hood curtained the sides of her face, covering all but a few wisps of golden-brown hair that were similar in color to his.

Nothing, not even the knowledge of what this female was, kept Jared from deciding that this vampire possessed a truly unusual kind of porcelain beauty. With fragile, delicate features, and because she was thin and so very pale, the female eyeing him back could have been described as ethereal.

She also looked young, and couldn't have been more than twenty-four when she became what she was. Jared supposed there was no way to tell how old she actually might be in terms of vampire years. Possibly immortality had rendered her ageless, at least on the outside.

"I don't suppose I actually resemble anything human," she mused, once again coming too close to Jared's thoughts for comfort. "The pale thing gives me away, right?"

"I haven't made up my mind about that," he replied. "Why don't you come closer and give me a better look?"

"I don't think that would be wise. Do you?"

Jared shrugged. "Do you have fangs?"

She nodded. "Standard equipment. Like your claws."

Jared glanced at the blade in her hand. "Are you hoping to use that blade on me?"

"I wouldn't think of it." She lifted the six-inch blade until it was level with her mouth. As she watched him over it, her dark eyes eerily reflected the glow of the polished metal.

"Actually," she added, "unlike you, I don't have much left in me that could be misconstrued for human."

Fascinated, still wary, Jared watched as she ran the blade across her lips, so that the blood staining it—his blood—transferred to her mouth. A pale pink tongue appeared from between her full lips, and his strange companion proceeded to flick the tip of that tongue across the edge of the blade as if it were an ice-cream cone.

Shudders of surprise and revelation rocked Jared. There was no mistake about this now, or about what species she belonged to. The female on the ledge actually was a vampire.

She was studying him as well, possibly looking for a reaction to what she had just done. When she didn't get that reaction, she tossed the blade to the street and jumped down after it. With the toe of her black boot, she kicked the knife into a storm drain that uselessly marked nearly every street in sunny L.A., and then turned to face him.

Jared raised an eyebrow, reminding her that he knew she had another knife tucked away somewhere.

She made no move to wipe the red stain from her mouth, and had not once shown her fangs. "I guess you can't be too surprised about me, since you also would know something about being other than human. Am I right, wolf?"

Jared couldn't take his gaze from her red-stained lips. The image of a pink tongue licking the blade clean looped through his mind. It was an image that should have turned him off and sent him packing. He found it odd that it hadn't. He truly was fascinated by what he was seeing. Here was yet another alternative to being human. As with him, this was a creature created from someone who had once been human, but continued on in a harsher version.

He found this vampire more intriguing than off-putting. She seemed to belong to the darkness around them, as if she were a shadow broken off from the rest. And she was a puzzle, because she hadn't gone for his jugular. Yet.

In fact, she might easily have been mistaken for just another follower of the Goth craze, with all that black makeup and her dark clothes. An eerily beautiful young rebel. Any male over the age of fifteen would have been intrigued by the way her outfit hugged her slim body, showing off each slender angle and slope. Hell, he was intrigued by those things.

Strange attractions should have stopped there, but the air of mystery surrounding the vampire added to a kind of seduction of the senses. About that also, there was no mistake whatsoever. She was a unique draw for a man who could no longer truly fit in with the world around him. She was someone to talk to during the long nighttime hours between sundown and dawn.

He wanted to talk, and wondered if any questions

about her species were taboo, or might annoy her if he got nosey. Jared decided he'd try one or two.

"Is the whole mysterious seduction thing part of a vampire's practiced mystique?" he asked. "Tops in a vampire's bag of tricks? The way you attract your prey?"

She returned a question. "You think I'm trying to seduce you?"

"Yes, in a subversive sort of way. Your otherness is fascinating."

Did he hear a soft chuckle of laughter? Jared could have sworn he did.

"You have no scent," he went on. "That lack of scent somehow carries its own fragrance."

"What does it smell like?" she asked.

"Night. All of the night scents rolled into one."

"Charming. Maybe I should bottle it. Make my fortune."

Jared wasn't finished with his evaluation. The vampire's silent vibe also spoke volumes about the things old novels about her species had spelled out so well. Possibly it was a vampire's almost mystical allure that allowed them to survive, and to exist on the sidelines of society in much the same way as he did.

She might not have been trying to seduce him into offering up more of his blood, but she was having a strange effect on him. Hell, he might even have been a little turned-on... which pointed directly to his lack of female companionship and the vow he had taken to never inadvertently infect another living person with the wolf virus after his own life-changing accident.

Besides the more obvious fact that she was dead, while he was voraciously alive, another big difference stood out like a beacon in Jared's mind. He had no desire to prey on the humans, while humans were, he supposed, a vampire's sole source of a food supply. Vampires fed from the life force of the living.

He squeezed his fist to staunch the trickle of blood from the knife wound, wondering if she had seen it.

"Might be time for you to go home, wolf," she suggested. "To me, you smell far too good, and like dessert."

She waited, as if daring him to turn his back.

"Why would I leave when this was just getting interesting?" Jared returned.

"Because I always was a sucker for dessert," she said. "FYI."

Jared didn't move.

"Well, then I'll do the honors," she concluded, turning from him. Speaking over a sharp-bladed shoulder, she added in a deeper tone, "Poaching is frowned upon, and you are trespassing in my territory. You've been doing so for quite some time."

The warning barely had time to settle before she vanished, moving so fast there was no residual imprint on the night. In disappearing so completely, it was as if she hadn't been there in the first place, though she'd left Jared with the barest hint of an idea that she had touched his face without him realizing it.

And if she could do that—getting close to him so easily and without his knowledge—then by letting his guard down for one single second meant he had fallen victim to her particular brand of seductive power, after all.

Trouble?

Hell. The word had just taken on a whole new meaning.

In this instance, *trouble* started a *V.*

Chapter

THREE

"Vampire."

In the past, Jared had never ever given a thought to the possibility of their existence. But then, he had been fairly tied up with his own personal shape-shifting dilemma.

He wondered if this female member of the vampire species was a decent version. At first glance, he hadn't noted anything noticeably undead about her. He understood that his interest in her had likely been tweaked because he was a man whose own life had been twisted against his will. In a way, Jared supposed this made them kindred spirits.

He knew very little about her kind, but did know one thing now, and that was how incredibly fast vampires were. Could she actually have touched him?

The fact that she had licked his blood from that blade should have left him feeling violated, offended, and sick. But none of those emotions had applied. Moreover, he had the feeling she had meant the gesture as a warning to him about the kind of powers she possessed. The only sick part about it was the fact that he had been mildly aroused by the witty repartee.

He knew he had been lonely, but hell. *Vampires?*

Unbelievably, after the initial tingle of danger had worn off, Jared felt hotter than usual, and for a werewolf, that was saying something. This vampire knew what he had become. She had not been afraid.

He didn't know what to call the sudden desire to go after her. Only his better judgment kept him nailed to the spot. It seemed to him they had connected in some way beyond two adversaries having a face-off in a dark alley. The minuscule blood transference from the knife to her mouth had seemed intimate, and almost sexual in nature.

He had been aroused, and therefore he was an idiot. Any idea he might have thought up about discovering more about that vampire and what lay beneath her black getup was wickedly unsound.

Jared turned his head. His skin began to ripple. His jaw twitched. As if the night's surprises so far hadn't been enough, his wolfish senses were warning him that more surprises were on tap. Visitors were coming, and quickly heading his way.

He eyed the street, inhaled deeply, sampled clues traveling in the air. Were these visitors human? *No.*

Missing heat signatures were now not only a forerunner of the vampire species, but a specific calling card for the creatures moving in. Vampires were coming, courtesy of the female on the ledge? Had she detained him for this reason? Long enough to call her pasty-faced pals?

Through half-closed eyes, Jared saw them. These vampires moved like an oncoming tide, flowing from shadow to shadow as if they were on skates. The atmosphere on the street grew heavier, as though something weighty was about to roll through— something that, like *her* and like him, didn't belong among Earth's regular populations.

Jared shook his head to clear it, and then shook it again. The air had an iron taste and a metallic odor. This, too, was unique. The vampire on the ledge had warned him about trespassing. Maybe others were coming to back that up.

One good leap took him onto the ledge the female had vacated, where he dropped to a crouch for a better view of the street. Muscles tense, jaw tight, he waited to see how quickly these newcomers would find him and what they would do when they did. Intuition, deep down inside him, suggested that these guys weren't coming for a chat.

So, if fiction had this right, and just in case his gut was also correct about this, Jared pondered how the undead could be dealt a final death blow, and what would take the dead down once and for all. Wooden stakes were hard to come by at the moment, as were metal crosses and vials of holy water. The only thing he had to fight them with was the strength of a werewolf's bare hands.

As if a fog had suddenly cleared, Jared saw them better. Three dark forms traveled within a camouflage of a black-gray mist. Dark things, hunched over. Oncoming air felt wet, heavy. The area had grown more silent than usual.

The sensation of having these vamps approach was unsettling. Jared waited, gearing up for a fight, knowing he'd have to tackle this if they were coming for him. But these vampires didn't stop beneath the ledge to look up at him. They rustled past without seeming to notice him at all.

All three of these guys scored high on the nonhuman test. Skeletal bodies, bleached faces, and other details rapidly filled in as they passed. Unlike the female he had met, these guys left Jared with an icy chill.

"Not after me then?" he whispered to the dark moving mist.

This was no time to relax, though. These beings, whoever they were and whatever kind of afterlife they served, were heading for the alley where Jared had left two startled human males not more than several minutes ago.

He hoped those idiots had cleared out.

What had the female said? He had been trespassing in her territory. Those words rang in Jared's ears now. Being a werewolf with a lot of muscle was one thing, but if those two humans had lingered, they would be in deep shit.

A symphony of sounds broke the silence suddenly. Human cries of fear and pain. Jared had never heard anything like them. Jumping from the ledge as deftly as its former occupant had, his body revved as he raced toward the clan, nest, hive, or whatever the hell best described a trio of vampires.

Maybe that female vampire hadn't called her friends to take care of him, and instead, their chat had been meant to isolate him from the people he had had left in that alley. If that were the case, who was the idiot now for not realizing he'd been played?

Jared reached the alley in seconds to find that all light had been drowned out by the blackness of the forms now occupying the small space. He couldn't see past the blur of black-on-black that made everything in that alley invisible to him, even with his special wolf vision.

There was movement, shouting, followed by a dreadful silence. The strange mist, damp and as dark as the night, met him as he stood on the edge of what could only have been described as a death zone.

Fuck. Yes. It was a death zone.

The alley stank of severed arteries, body parts, and blood spatter. He was all too familiar with the foulness of that odor, and remembered how his body had been chewed up less than a block down the street.

Two tours in Afghanistan had sealed the smell of blood and bodily damage permanently into his databanks, and due to his werewolf senses being magnified a hundred times beyond the normal human range, the smell in that alley made him issue an inhuman howl.

The weight of that howl burned his throat. It was a throwback to the nature from which all wolves sprang, and served to attract the attention of the dark moving forms.

Black mist separated into two streams. One of those streams curled around him, climbed up his legs, clawed at this coat. The other black stream curved to the side, bypassing the growling werewolf in his man form at the head of the alley as if the beings that mist hid had intentions other than engaging him for a meal or a fight.

Jared couldn't quite reach the moonlight in order to increase his odds of survival. As the black mist crawled up his limbs, he felt a hand wrap around his wrist. Startled by the strength of that hand's grip, Jared stilled as a voice whispered in his ear with a cool, familiar tone.

"One more howl, wolf, will do it. Weres and vampires are old enemies. The wildness of the animal in your blood does not interest us."

Shocked over hearing this particular voice again, Jared howled loudly in reaction. The vocalization set his teeth on edge. Amplified by the alley's close walls, the sound echoed on and on as if the alley were endless.

Still, he couldn't step backward and into the moonlight in order to free his wolf. Gusts of fetid air blew across his face, bringing an urge to gag. But for one brief moment, as the mist began to thin, Jared clearly saw the kind of destruction vampires had caused here.

They weren't just monsters. These were bloodsucking freaks.

Their appearance was nothing remotely like the female version he had met on the ledge. These vampires were male, tall, emaciated, with red eyes and terrible yellow protruding canines that had just proved how extremely dangerous they were.

One of the vampires stood beside him. Two more huddled against the old brick walls to his right. *Christ!* They were lapping the blood from those walls with their lips and tongues, cleaning up the area in a grotesque manner that made Jared's insides quake with disgust.

His stomach turned over. His head swam with the beastly images in front of him. This was appalling, wrong, horrifying. And real.

Pushed by emotion, Jared stumbled backward. His claws ripped through his fingertips, long, curved, sharp. His shoulders began to broaden.

He had to do something to stop the nightmare.

Without managing a full shape-shift, Jared swiped at the vampire standing beside him, missing the lightning-fast creature as it dodged to the side. The hand that had been gripping his wrist tightened. The familiar voice spoke again.

"No, wolf. Don't engage them. It's over. Let this go."

It was *her* voice. The vampire female he had met earlier was offering him advice on how to deal with the others.

I found you beautiful... he wanted to say to her. *Now look.* This scene was far from acceptable. Jared was ashamed that he had been intrigued by such a creature. Her clan had found and slaughtered the ruffians he had let go. They were killers. Supernatural murderers.

His howl of protest, still echoing in the alley, seemed to have done something. The mist hugging his legs unfurled. When he turned his head to locate the female who had whispered to him, he found no one.

The blackness that had infiltrated the alley quickly cleared away. No members of the walking undead lapped at the brick. There was no evidence that anything bad had taken place in the damn alley. Every scrap of tonight's slaughter had been erased.

Jared stood there alone, only partially shifted and too stunned to be angry.

Sirens roared in the distance, but weren't coming closer. Overhead, a helicopter whirred, heading east. He was the only one that knew about what had happened here, and who could he have told if he had wanted to? Who would believe a werewolf anyway, even if he had been a detective before his injuries had forced him to take some time to himself?

Surely his old buddies in law enforcement would question his reasons for being on this street, at this hour? They hadn't been able to find his attacker a year ago, and would assume he'd now gone vigilante if he called this in.

"I believe a thank-you is order," a voice remarked, startling Jared again.

"A thank-you?" Jared tossed back as he searched the tight space for a visual. "For playing along with your scheme?"

"For saving you the trouble of having to put up a fight."

"You? Saved me?" He didn't sound the least bit contrite.

"Did you assume your claws did the trick?" she tossed back. "All I needed was a sample of your blood, which you provided. Blood sends a message. Your blood on my lips marked you."

"Marked me as ignorant and gullible?"

A rustling noise came from his right. Jared traced

the sound to the darkest part of the alley.

The vampire's voice was in soft mode when she spoke again. "It marked you as off-limits to everyone but me."

Another shudder passed through Jared, but he remained undaunted by her remark.

"So, I'm to be your next meal? Is that the way you're expecting this to go?" He took another backward step that again brought him within an inch of the moonlight.

"You do go to extremes," she complained, as if the pictures in his mind of fighting fanged beasts were hers as well. "And you have quite an imagination."

"What do you mean by that whole marking thing?"

"It means I was your backup here. No army necessary. Just one little..."

"Fanged bodyguard?"

After he uttered that remark, a moment of silence passed. The sirens and the helicopter were long gone. Jared thought his voice sounded flat.

The vampire finally spoke again, her voice faint and far-off. "See you soon, wolf. If you dare to come looking, you'll know where to find me."

He didn't ask her to wait, or demand to know what the hell she was talking about. He was somehow marked because of the blood she had licked from the damn blade? What did being marked by a vampire mean, in terms of keeping other vampires off him in this alley?

He had been after another kind of monster here, one with canines and claws, and look what had turned up—a female with fangs and a disturbingly cryptic sense of humor.

"Can you hear me?" Jared called out, figuring she could, and supposing the vampire might be watching him even now without him knowing it. The pressure in his ears hadn't gone away. He was curiously breathless and felt like his lungs were being squeezed.

"You'll need to explain," he said, taking that last step back toward the street.

When a shower of moonlight hit him, the sensation was like jumping into a lake of cold water. One shudder in reaction to the change in his body temperature, and Jared completed his shape-shift.

C h a p t e r

FOUR

From her new vantage point, Kit observed every move the werewolf made with careful consideration.

She saw moonlight cover him in a wash of silver. The shudder that rocked the werewolf also rocked her. She had to be careful now that they were blood-bound. Chances were good that if the werewolf couldn't see her yet, he might be able to sense her lurking among the dark spaces. That's the way blood marking went, and it was a neat trick for the beings willing to undergo a heightened awareness of each other.

And actually, it was her blood connection to the wolf that had helped her to save his very commendable ass.

Well... okay. She might have done that anyway.

Fascinated by how a body could adapt to such a larger shape, Kit stared as the wolf's transformation from man to his wilder side happened. If she still had breath, she would have sighed in appreciation of the process and how painful it must have been.

His spine had been the first thing to alter. After a series of pops and rattles, the wolf's back lengthened and curved, forcing muscle and sinew to stretch and reshape. His chest expanded. Ribs cracked. Shoulders, already broad in the man, widened.

More muscle mounded. His height extended slightly. When her wolf straightened up, having mastered the pain in silence, his hands again had spouted six-inch claws. The face she had liked so much had elongated, making his light blue eyes seem larger, darker.

The leather coat, roomy enough to take on this change, was now filled out by a being that was neither wolf nor man, but half of both things. He was a beast, but magnificent. She'd have told him so, if she had dared. But there was more to note.

His features were still sculpted and mostly aquiline, retaining a lot of their former characteristics. Angles and hollows lined up in all the right places. Burnished brown locks, worn to the length of his collar before his transformation, seemed longer now, and the scent of the moonlight-drenched locks scattered when he shook his head.

"Do you know I'm here, wolf?" Kit whispered. "Just you and me? Here, now?"

She craned her neck. The desire to speak to him was nearly getting the better of her. She'd have told him more about herself if they had met under other circumstances. She would have explained that she didn't belong to any nasty nest or coven and that she had never seen those vampire freaks in the alley before tonight. None of those freaks knew anything about her, other than the fact that she also was a vampire, and therefore was to be left alone.

She was different from the bloodsuckers in

many ways, she'd tell this wolf if he stuck around long enough. She was a vampire with feelings, wants, needs, and thirsted for more than blood. Those other desires are what separated her from the rest.

"Would you believe me, I wonder?"

Of course, she couldn't engage with him again so soon. In fact, it would have been better for her to have left him alone in the first place. She had exposed herself to a stranger, but her wolf was also a being that no longer belonged to the human race. He would know something about secrets. Maybe he would understand hers.

"It has been a long time since I've stepped out of the dark to reveal myself to anyone, let alone a living, warm-blooded being," Kit murmured, swallowing the impulse to say those words loud enough for him to hear.

In the end, caution is what kept her from doing or saying anything. She was a vampire. This wolf wasn't like her and never could be… just as she couldn't become a wolf, like him. Fate couldn't twist things both ways.

But she wanted him.

Kit wanted to be like him.

It felt like she already knew him, since he had been coming here for so many months, diligently standing guard as if he might be desperate to find something that remained hidden from him. She knew his scent, his expressions, and how careful he was to keep the werewolf locked inside its cage.

He was searching for something special. Waiting for something to happen. Kit could venture a guess as to what that was. Wasn't she here for the same reason? Didn't she hope to find the bloodsucker that had fed on her and had stolen her life away? The monster that had bled her, forced her to look Death in the eye, and turned her into something obscene?

Only an outside disturbance had interrupted the bloodsucker's feeding frenzy in time to preserve one lingering piece of her old self. Her soul.

"That interruption was you, wolf," Kit whispered, still observing the guy. "So if I need to thank anyone for not becoming exactly like those yellow-fanged creeps in the alley, those thanks go to you."

In light of that, how could she have allowed the freaks that had turned up tonight to have any part of him? Hurt him more?

Kit nodded. "Turnabout is fair play, right wolf? You helped me, and I returned the favor. I suppose that makes us even."

The werewolf was still standing there, motionless, silent, looking to have been carved in stone. Kit moved to the rim of the rooftop hoping for a better look at his face. Even fully morphed, she liked what she saw. Through the particles of his blood now swimming in her bloodstream, she was aware of what he was feeling.

"Not your fault... what happened to those hoodlums on the alley. Hunger rules vampires, and most people stay away from this area these days. How were you to know a black wave would show up, wolf? I didn't."

The werewolf was feeling guilty for the death of the humans that had tried to hustle him. He possessed an intrinsic need to help others, which made him a good guy. A werewolf good guy.

Kit was sorry that hunger ruled her and that she and this werewolf didn't have more in common. She detested the cravings that ravaged her system, and she desperately wanted her former life back… which in the end, was too fucking bad.

"Where do we go from here?" she asked in a voice that wouldn't carry even if this werewolf's hearing was exceptional.

Her voice was a tool. Her whisper, in his ear, would have the effect of a command. But she didn't want him that way. She didn't plan to use the connection to him that she had set in place by sampling his blood. He didn't deserve that.

Still, the wolf had been interested in her without using vamp hexes on him. And if he had looked at her right then, it would have been tough for her to remain hidden from the gorgeous loner for that reason alone.

"Do you also feel our bond, wolf?"

Would he have a clue as to why his interest in her wouldn't fade as long as she was in the area?

"Blood did that. Your blood on my lips."

I have caused this connection, but my intentions were good. I swear I just wanted to keep other bloodsuckers off you.

Kit felt a connection to the monster that had bitten her in much the same way as she felt this wolf's liveness. Blood to blood was a bond that went beyond life and death. The fiend that had killed her had left an indelible imprint on her soul that the monster hadn't been able to erase. She would be able to separate him from all other bloodsuckers if he came around, and sincerely hoped he would show up someday.

"And now I have done a similar thing to you, wolf. I have pinned you to my radar."

The wolf's presence was heady, strong, rich. The vibes he gave off were unique, and a lot like soul food for a starved dead girl. He was a reminder of what she had lost, times ten. The wolf was alive, warm, masculine, and fragrant.

After a pause, Kit added a last thing under her breath. "If I had turned out like the others, maybe I wouldn't hurt so badly, deep down inside, for things I can never have. Maybe having a soul is actually a burden, and I don't owe you anything for helping to preserve mine."

She blinked slowly to get a grip on herself, searching for reasons to leave the wolf alone. Differences? Hell, there were too many to count. Did that seem to matter at the moment?

He probably slept in a bed in an airy loft downtown. He probably walked in the sunlight among the people of this city, ate in restaurants, and drove a car. For the most part, and minus a full moon, he would fit in.

While she…

She hardly slept at all, and had to be wary even then. She had to retreat to the darkest places while the sun was up, like a wounded animal in hiding. She had to fight the urge to bite the first thing she came into contact with when nighttime hours rolled around, and make do with sipping from the veins of humans and beasts sprung from a lesser gene pool. Drunks. Drug-addicts. Sick people. She had vowed never to hurt the others.

Truly, she shouldn't be grateful to this wolf for the unknowing part he had played in her afterlife. Looking at him hurt. Owing him anything hurt.

So, what does that make me, wolf?

Where does that leave me?

Where does that leave us?

Kit half expected the wolf to answer those questions, though she had taken great care to hide herself from him.

"Some other time, then," she said, staring at the dried red flecks on her colorless knuckles that were remnants of his blood. "Blood is my bane, wolf, while moonlight is yours. In the end, we're both monsters, you know."

Uncomfortable with her thoughts, Kit glanced up at the moon before gazing again at the magnificent werewolf only then beginning to move.

Wanting to follow him, reach him, was only part of her new dilemma. The rest of her desires were never to be addressed. She would let him go. Let him leave.

Hurry, before I change my mind.

Ingesting his blood had been folly, and way too intimate. This wolf's life fluid was creating chaos inside her and stirring things up.

Kit's mind again issued a stern warning.

Let him go. Let him leave.

But the rest of her wasn't fully onboard with those suggestions. The rest of her wanted to know him better. Wanted more. Wanted him, and what he had to offer.

He turned from the alley. After scanning the area and perceiving no threat, the big werewolf shuddered back to his man shape as if merely throwing off a chill. He took five big breaths, then a sixth, and uttered a groan before beginning to walk, careful to keep close to the buildings in order to avoid a repeat performance of adopting an alternate identity.

She was going to lose him. At least for now.

Inside Kit's chest, where her heart once beat, came an unusual fluttering sensation. She closed her eyes briefly before blinking up at the moonlight.

Then, in direct opposition to her inner warnings, Kit followed the wolf, leaping agilely from rooftop to rooftop until he reached the intersection at the end of the block. He paused there and glanced over a broad shoulder, as though he felt her presence, before he continued on.

Let him go, Kit's conscience shouted.

Don't interfere.

The urge to speak to him was outrageous, as was the impulse to call him back.

"We're even," she muttered. "I've paid you back tonight for saving what was left of me out here a year ago. You didn't know about that, did you? I never told you."

Although she wasn't sure she liked the result of his interference, and felt as if she'd been stuck between two worlds, neither in or out of either of them, Kit knew that it was just too damn late to bring this up. So she studied the wolf's retreat with a heavy heart... though she didn't really have a working heart.

If I never see you again, so much the better.

But deep down inside her, Kit knew that all the protests weren't true and that there would be a next time. Another meeting. More conversations. Her wolf would come back, seek her out. Interest in her had been his downfall, just as her interest in him might prove to be hers. She had seen a flare of lust in his eyes and had reveled in the knowledge that he wanted her as badly as she wanted him.

After clutching her chest, striving to feel the missing beats, Kit pushed back her hood to feel what was left of the wind on her face. Somehow words like *soul* and *emotion* had become intertwined. She desperately wanted a further connection with this guy, however unlikely that was.

He was still visible from where she crouched. Well over six feet of perfectly corded muscle moved with the slow grace of his ancient animal relations and the confidence of a prince—head held high, shoulders back, arms loose at his sides. That stuff colored the surface—the parts of him other people would see. Yet she perceived the wolf's tension.

Beneath his black coat, his body was taut with readiness, in case there were other surprises in store. His formidable focus caused another man to move out of his way.

He didn't pause again to look up or behind him. If he felt her hovering like a shadow, he didn't search the roofline. Kit shook off a wave of sadness. He would soon be out of sight.

Both of her hands trembled slightly. The back

of her neck tingled. She moved her lips to quell her anxiousness over the losing the guy.

"You will come back. You will come back here, my fine werewolf, and I'll be waiting."

C h a p t e r

FIVE

Jared paced back and forth from his bedroom to the living room enough times to wear out spots in the floor. He was antsy and needed to run, but didn't dare set foot outside of his home again. By allowing the waning moonlight to reach him out there, he knew he'd wind up back near that blasted alley, and *her.*

His wolf parts wanted a rerun with the vampire. So did the rest of him. He just wasn't sure that would be a good idea. Vampires were bad news.

The usual "breathe deeply and calm down" sentiments weren't working, though. A strikingly pale face filled his thoughts. The vampire's testy voice echoed over and over inside his head. A long shower hadn't washed away the thoughts of her, and neither had inner conversations with himself about the merits of common sense.

After several more minutes of pacing, Jared climbed onto the bed. Then he got up again. Sleep was going to be impossible. His mind was experiencing a whiteout.

For the fiftieth time, Jared peered out of the front window of his second story apartment, telling himself—no, actually chastising himself—for behaving as if he had been hypnotized by a pair of dark, haunting eyes. The female on that ledge had fangs, for Christ's sake. She had no pulse. He was supposed to be protecting people from the monsters, not having midnight meet-and-greets with them.

Swearing a string of oaths, Jared looked outside again half expecting to see the vampire standing at the curb, not really sure what he would have done if she had been there.

Damn it, he almost wished she had followed him home so that he could tell her to get out of his mind and send her back to the shadows from which she had sprung. He had wooden chairs in the dining room. He could break off a leg and use that for a vamp-fighting weapon.

Each glance outside confirmed that he was acting like an idiot. No vamp chick stood on the sidewalk. She wasn't calling to him and didn't know where he lived. The phrases he thought he heard her whisper were nothing more than his awkward imagination at work, and certainly had nothing to do with wishful thinking.

As the clock ticked annoyingly and more minutes passed, Jared grew impatient with his own restlessness. His system had been disturbed too many times tonight, and that was never good. The moon was weaker now, but still in the sky. His wolf parts sensed that moon's exact location. Once the werewolf had been unleashed, it always wanted to make a comeback, and the werewolf was pushy.

"Okay. I give up."

He leaned over to pick his pants up off the floor,

already knowing this was going to be a very bad idea.

"You win."

Tugging on his jeans and boots, grabbing his coat, Jared opened the door to his balcony and stepped outside. His neighbors wouldn't see him, and even if they did, they'd understand that detectives sometimes kept late hours. What they didn't need to know was that this detective was so much more than a man with a badge, and that he had taken up a vigilante's method of justice afterhours in his hunt for monsters.

"I'll be waiting..."

The vampire's voice was driving him mad. He had no other recourse but to see what the hell she wanted from him. And if that turned out to be blood, well, let her try to take it.

Determined to stop the internal chatter, Jared reached for the railing and swung himself over. He landed softly on the sidewalk. No one else was around to witness this death-defying leap. Straightening up, and without the necessary means to keep hidden, the moonlight found him as easily if someone had nailed him with a searchlight.

Liquid light seeped through the open sides of his coat, bringing first a chill to his bare chest, then a quick flush of heat. More light melted over his face as he accepted the moon's treacherous kiss. Muscles twitched. His teeth snapped shut. Bones snapped and realigned. Ligaments strained against their connections. Accepting a sharp stab of pain that nearly brought him to his knees, and for the second time that night, Jared's human-like semblance melted away.

*

Kit's head came up. She got to her feet, ignoring the hunger pangs twisting her insides. Something was up, and it didn't involve the prospect of finding dinner.

The swirl of awareness hitting her was an acknowledgment of a wish about to be fulfilled. Her wolf was coming back.

In the distance, she heard a howl. The kind of sound wild animals made. Her wolf was angry.

She climbed down one story of the building she clung to and slid over pieces of loosened concrete tiles. Balancing on a narrow window ledge, Kit scanned the street below her hoping she was right about the wolf's return. Because when had a doomed soul like hers ever been granted a wish, or deserved a bit of good fortune?

When a dark figure turned the corner, Kit anxiously waited. It wasn't necessary for her to see that shadowy figure up close in order to know who it was. His movement had *wolf* written all over it.

Her body began to quake with a mixture of pleasure and disbelief as she recognizing that wolf in ways no mortal would have understood. Gripping the building's ornate trim, she lowered herself down to within jumping range of the ground and hesitated without taking the final leap. What could she expect? How angry would he be?

Their uncanny connection might have gotten the better of him, dictating how this was to go down, but really, most of the attraction they felt had more to do with being able to get close to another anomaly without fear or regret, she supposed.

The werewolf stopped beneath the spot where she stood. He was frighteningly large and terribly formidable, but Kit didn't have to worry about those things since he was the lesser evil here in the monster lineup.

"What do you want?" Kit called out, feeling all riled up inside and as if she had already taken a stake to the chest. "I don't suppose you can speak when you're all furred up?"

The term "furred up" didn't actually suit this guy. The only hair she could see was on his head—a shiny brown mane that swung across the collar of his coat when he turned.

She crouched on the narrow ledge, ready to spring, and said testily, "Maybe you can nod your head once for yes, and twice for no? No, Wait. Shake your head for no."

Her tone was purposefully clipped and harsh. Now that he was here, now that he had come back, Kit wasn't entirely sure how to handle the situation. They were on opposing sides of the afterlife spectrum. There was no way they could ever be a couple, so what had she expected?

When the werewolf remained motionless, Kit figured he was trying to scope her out, see what made vampires tick. She actually felt his mind attempt to probe hers. Yet if that was his objective, he'd be waiting a very long time.

"I know what I am," she said. "And you know what I am. So, what now? Why are you here? Since you're not a normal member of the general public either, and we've already talked about the kinds of strengths we possess, what sort of face-off can we expect?"

His low growl shook the crumbling ledge she crouched upon.

Kit stood up. "I'm not afraid of you, so you can lose the growling routine. It's hard for me to read you when you're wolfed up, let alone carry on a conversation. Can you change back?"

The wolf raised his face. His eyes trained on her. When she met that gaze, Kit felt the return of that odd internal flutter she had experienced the first time she'd seen this guy. His eyes were very human in his changed face. It was possible for her to see the human in this outline.

"Will you try to kill me?" she asked. "Is that why you've come back?"

The beast shook his head. Taking a giant step to escape the moonlight, he merged with the shadows pooling at the junction where the building met the sidewalk. His reverse shape-shift sounded like a chunk of raw meat being slapped down on a hard surface.

When her guest didn't immediately emerge from the shadows, Kit jumped to the sidewalk.

His voice broke the silence. "What do you want from me?"

"I'm not certain how to answer that question without sounding pathetically unvampire-like," she replied.

Even in his human form, this guy was two heads taller than she was and so obviously, deliciously, alive, Kit would have been attracted to his warmth alone.

As he waited for her to explain her remark, Kit tried to decide if she would oblige.

"I thought we might be friends," she eventually said. *Friends* wasn't the right word to describe what she wanted from this guy, however. Maybe she didn't know how to describe that. Possibly it would have been absurd to try any explanation when she really didn't know what she wanted from him. At the moment, company is what she craved. His company.

"Some of us sleep," he said, inching toward where she stood. "You've disturbed mine."

"I sleep," she returned, failing to add how unapologetic she felt for disturbing his slumber.

"From what I've heard, vampires have opposite sleep schedules," he remarked.

"You've been around a lot of vampires then?"

"Only one."

Kit nodded. "You mean me."

"What do you want?" he repeated.

"Would you like the truth?"

"The truth would be good."

"Warmth," Kit said, quickly adding, "Sunlight. Green grass. Vacations beside a lake of clear water. Tanned skin. Breath would be nice. And heartbeats. A soft bed in an airy room is on my wish list, as is strong coffee and chocolate dessert. Those are just a few of the things I miss."

Her answer disturbed the wolf. Kit heard his pulse spike. She could almost see that pulse in his neck.

Knowing where her focus had gone, he said, "I'm sorry."

"For my little problem of being unable to attain any of those things?"

He came closer, carefully edging the moonlit sidewalk. "I'm sorry for anyone who has no choice in becoming something other than one hundred percent human."

Kit rode out a few seconds of thought before muttering, "Amen to that."

"You said *unvampire-like*. Vampires aren't supposed to confess to missing things they once had?" he asked thoughtfully.

"Takes the edge off the mystery somewhat, don't you think?" Kit replied.

He nodded.

That nod of understanding further softened Kit's stance on confessions and vulnerability. She had to consciously keep herself from leaning into the shadows and into him, seeking more empathy and body heat. Her world was a cold one. She was so often chilled to the bone these days.

"You wanted to talk?" he asked her. "Be friends? That's it?"

"Do you have many friends these days, wolf? If so, how many of them have heard you howl?" Kit countered.

"Not a single one knows about what I've become," he admitted, adding after a beat, "You didn't ask for this kind of existence? Didn't seek it out?"

"Who in their right mind would? But it is what it is. We deal because what's the alternative? Isn't it the same for you?"

Again, Kit noted the wolf's inner disturbance over her answer. Seeming to forget about the moonlight, he took another short step toward her.

She did not back away.

"Do you have any particular reason for claiming this particular area of the city?" he asked.

The big guy was frightfully insightful. Kit wondered what he did in his day job. He had a soft way with interrogations and appeared to be truly interested in what she might say. She also wondered whether werewolves could handle being around a lot of people, or if their inner wildness made them loners. She contemplated whether he might have a girlfriend, a thought that brought on another internal flutter as Kit closed her lips tightly over her fangs.

He spoke again. "Not many people venture here. I would assume it would be slim pickings in this area for a hungry vampire."

"And for a werewolf? What brings you back month after month?" she countered.

"Protecting bad areas is what I do. With the kind of strength being part wolf gives me, I don't worry too much about being on my own."

"Why here?" Kit pressed. "You return here over and over each time there's a full moon overhead. Is there a reason you haunt this place?"

"How long have you been watching me?" he asked.

"For almost a year." Kit said this truthfully, seeing no reason to lie now that he knew about her and about what she was, and because they had shared with each other about their particular brands of abnormalities.

When the wolf sighed, his breath came to Kit as warm stream of lightly scented air that easily could have undermined her will to hold out against any show of mental weakness. Was he a kindhearted soul? She imaged so.

"I'm a vampire," she said, as if he'd get the true meaning behind the word if she repeated it a few more times. "I troll the dark spaces where good people fear to tread."

"And yet you are unlike the others I met here earlier tonight. So, what makes you different?"

"I suppose it's because I still have a soul."

"Those other fanged creatures don't?" the wolf asked.

"The others are bloodsuckers, plain and simple. They exist only to feed, and serve no other purpose."

The wolf leaned toward her and lowered his voice. "You don't feed on others?"

"Only for sport," Kit replied with a healthy dose of sarcasm, avoiding the wolf's probing gaze.

"I thought we were to tell the truth," he reminded her.

"I've just confessed to having a soul. That isn't good enough?"

When he nodded, his shaggy hair curtained the sides of his handsome, chiseled face. His coat was open, showing off the perfect musculature of his broad chest and enviable abs, which meant that he had been in a hurry to get here and hadn't taken the time to get fully dressed.

The thought of this wolf in the buff gave Kit an unexpected shiver of pleasure. Also pleasurable was the budding idea that there was no Mrs. Werewolf or casual female sleepover, facts that had allowed him to return to her tonight.

"I come back here because this is where I was born," he confessed, taking the initiative to further the conversation. "This alley is where the man became something else. I come back here to make sure what happened to me doesn't happen to anyone else."

Kit wasn't surprised by the honesty of his statement. Yet the truth of it stung her, as did the casualness of the way the wolf had mentioned something so personal. Empathy swelled within her. She knew this kind of pain all too well.

She said, "I hang around this street for the same reason. This is where I met with a nasty pair of fangs and had my throat torn out. This is the location where my blood was drained and I woke up to darkness beyond the reach of any kind of light."

Until now, she almost added. *Until meeting you changed that.*

It seemed to Kit now that fate had brought two unsettled souls together so they could commiserate. In essence, she and this wolf were ghosts gathered around the location where their former lives had been taken or altered.

"I'm sorry for what happened to you," he said.

"So am I," Kit seconded.

"How do you know you have a soul?" he asked.

"I wouldn't be standing here, talking to you, if I didn't."

"Is that unusual? Retaining your soul?"

"Highly unusual, by the way things look around here. And I'm pretty sure that retaining my soul was a mistake."

She didn't have to tell the whole truth, Kit decided. She didn't owe her life story to this guy, no matter how attracted to him or in need of his company she was. Nor did she want to be beholden to him when she wasn't certain that keeping her soul was a good thing.

Nevertheless, she owed him the soul she had told him about, and she had this wolf to thank for the way things had turned out. He was responsible for her being here now, and chatting with him as if she were still human. The fact that they both were abominations was the glue keeping them pinned to this spot.

"I want to find that bastard," she said. "I want to find the monster that killed me."

The wolf nodded. "Someday the freak who changed my life will venture back here, and I'll be waiting."

"Maybe your monster and my monster will come here together and we can clean up the street in one big sweep," Kit said, feeling her hard-won self-control about maintaining some distance from this guy start to slip even more than it already had. His incredible heat was one thing. His acceptance of her condition was quite another. They were conversing as if they were people. Like they were anyone.

"So, we both wait here, hoping for justice," he said.

"Revenge?" Kit suggested.

"I'm not sure revenge is what I'm seeking," he said.

"Then you're a better ghost than I am."

The wolf continued to study her. Kit found his gaze disconcerting and way too personal. If her willpower slipped another notch in the wrong direction, would he be able to see down into that soul? See how vulnerable she actually felt?

"I don't need your blood," she told him, hoping that wasn't what he was anticipating. "I don't want anything like that from you."

"Why did you call to me, and how did you do it? Since we're to be friends, why not tell me that?"

"Your particles are inside me, thanks to the blood on that knife. I know what you taste like. I know your essence. Somehow this makes it easier for me to read you. But I have believed for some time that we are kindred spirits."

The wolf glanced away, then back.

Kit went on. "The alternative, of course, is that you just wanted to come back here, all on your own."

She watched him mull that over. He was fairly decent at hiding his expressions, but a small twitch at the corner of his mouth gave him away. He would have returned even if she hadn't wished for that so hard.

"Anyway, you don't taste all that good," she said. "I've had better."

He smiled.

Kit's chest flutter became a shudder that rocked her stance. Yet what was the point of all that fluttering, other than enjoying a minor flirtation on a dark street? Big reminder. There was no future to be had here. To think there could be was madness.

"Possibly we're both tied to this place until we get the kind of justice we seek, and then we'll be free from the search for freedom. Having two of us with the same goal might make it twice as lucky that might happen," the wolf proposed.

Kit blinked slowly. "I despise optimists, wolf."

He rallied quickly. "What would you call beings like us who wait here month after month hoping an old nemesis will come along?"

"I'd call them persistent."

Her wolf smiled again with a dazzling display of humor's ability to lighten the darkest places. The side-effect of his expression was how completely that smile had captured the part of her soul reserved for a little thing called *hope*.

"I suppose you might wait for your monster longer. Aren't vampires immortal?" he asked.

"I'd find a way to kill myself if it took forever for the wheels of justice to turn my way. Besides, I'm not sure about the whole immortal thing, and can't imagine what that might mean. No one has challenged my right to exist like this. No one showed up to try to end my existence, so what do I know about how long my existence might continue?"

Real hell, Kit thought, would be to continue on night after night, year after year... like this.

She eyed the wolf seriously. "Will an optimist challenge me?"

He shook his head. "I believe, since I'm pretty far from normal myself, that scenario would make me a hypocrite."

It was her turn to smile. Only then did Kit remember about her fangs, and what his reaction to them might be.

C h a p t e r

SIX

Jared wasn't thrown off-balance by the first sight of his companion's razor-sharp teeth. After all, he sometimes had ten lethal claws to deal with.

The vampire stood very close to him now in a thin wedge of darkness squeezed between weak shafts of moonlight. They were almost touching. One step in any direction would bathe him in light and signal a shape-shift. The vampire would probably know that. So the question Jared asked himself was what she planned to do next?

"You're not scared?" She closed her lips over the fangs.

He stared at her mouth. "Not in the least."

Honestly, Jared supposed this vampire might have been the only other so-called person on the planet who'd have dared to face down a werewolf in close quarters. He was relieved to find that someone who knew his secret wasn't backing away from him.

She looked up at him with her eyes narrowed. "Do you mind if I touch you, wolf?"

"That depends."

"On whether I lied about not wanting to suck your blood?"

"Since you mentioned that wolf blood didn't taste very good, I'd be wondering more about what taking that bite would say about you."

"It's your warmth that draws me," she confessed. "You have no idea how cold it can get in my world."

"Would you like my coat?"

She shook her head. "It doesn't work like that."

"Clothes can't warm you?"

"Nothing can warm me really, except…"

Without thinking, Jared reached for the vampire and drew her to him, granting her wish for warmth. He was mildly surprised that she felt like every other person—solid, real, flesh and bone—though her skin was icy against his bare chest.

If this was a lie and a ploy for her to try to bite him, he'd be ready. Merely a few inches in any direction to reach the moonlight, and that would be that.

Still, he couldn't remember the last time he had been with a woman of any species, and it felt good to hold one. After what had happened to him, and what he had become, he feared contact of any kind.

Before that fateful night on this blasted street he'd had plenty of partners, so his forced celibacy hadn't been easy or welcome. Just how much he had missed female companionship came home to him now, and getting up close and personal with this vampire didn't alter that feeling.

If he let himself go, Jared could almost have believed that he and this vampire were just a man and a woman sharing a moment that was new, unique, and incredibly intense. He actually wanted to believe that.

When he encircled her slender body with both arms, she didn't protest. Her arms dangled at her sides as if she either didn't know what to do with them, or didn't trust herself to accept his embrace.

After a few awkward moments, she relaxed enough to rest her head against his shoulder, as if she'd begun to thaw. Jared mentally calculated the inches those fangs of hers might have to travel to reach the artery in his neck, and waited for her to make her move. But she didn't make it. She stood there, seemingly content to soak up his body heat. After shivering once, she burrowed closer to him.

Every inch of her body was female, Jared discovered. She had small breasts and a taut belly. With her chest pressed to his chest and her hips against his, his arousal returned. Although having a female plastered to him was only a distant memory, it was a fond one. He might be a werewolf, but he still had a male's needs.

When the willowy vampire looked up at him again, he released her. As their gazes met and held, Jared's inner wolf stirred—those parts of him that might have preferred getting down and dirty with a vampire on the sidewalk. Instead of being anxious, his inner wildness appreciated the intimacy of their shared moment of madness.

Although he couldn't read the vampire's expression, Jared thought he saw puzzlement cross her features in a flash that was there and gone. Her big eyes blinked twice, breaking contact.

Did he see dampness glistening there?

Hell, even a big bad werewolf was a sucker for tears.

When she spoke again, it was a series of curses. "Damn it. Damn everything. Damn you."

A brand new awareness ticked the insides of Jared's throat, one that that had nothing to do with male and female bonding.

He turned his head.

His companion spoke first. Identifying the newest wave of sensation she announced, "More monsters are coming."

Jared followed her gaze to the street. "Vampires?"

"Only one," she said, slipping sideways to peer around the corner.

"The one?" Jared asked.

He ignored the blank expression she offered him. This edgy little vampire was excited and couldn't hide that from him. Her whole demeanor had changed.

"Is it time to meet your Maker?" he whispered.

Her big eyes flicked to him and back to the corner.

"Well then, let's go and see," he suggested as he took that last step into the moonlight. "Maybe one of us can get our wish."

*

Kit moved in a flash toward the street without bothering to check for the werewolf because she felt every move he made as if she were the one making it. Without more than a few hundred words spoken between them, she knew he would have her back no matter what kind of threat might appear. He had offered warmth to a cold soul and hadn't said one word about her fangs.

With her lips parted and her anxiety levels high, Kit's fangs sliced into her lower lip, cutting deep. An unwelcomed wetness tricked over her chin, but she didn't wipe it away. A tight ball of anger was growing inside her. So were feelings that no self-respecting vampire should have had for anyone, let alone a stranger from another species.

She had shown the wolf her underbelly, that vulnerable spot she loathed. If he wanted to use that against her, he now had all the ammunition he needed to do so.

Behind her, the werewolf growled. The sheer force of the menace in the sound he made bolstered her fierce sense of justice. She was a vampire, for fuck's sake. What more could happen to her if the monster that had made her a vampire actually showed up again, when the damage had already been done? Conversely, what did she have to live for, or look forward to, except more years of hiding in the darkness and the gut-wrenching, ever-present desire for blood?

There was no *what-if* here. None at all. The freak that had turned her into a freak had to be taken down.

Still, Kit's purpose for continuing to take up space on Earth suddenly seemed to have been divided. Tackling that nasty bloodsucking bastard had been her primary objective and what she had waited for on this damn street, all this time. Seriously, how could she hope to have anything that remotely resembled a reasonable afterlife spent with the gorgeous werewolf most women would have given their eye-teeth to get into bed?

She had to nix her growing feelings for the hot-blooded wolf hunk and move on. She had to keep watch for Bloodsucker Zero and take out her frustrations on him. Maintaining balance was paramount. Balance and perspective.

The werewolf's second growl tore through the dark. Kit's spine stiffened as she coasted to the center of the street and stopped with her hands on her hips. The werewolf stopped beside her, close enough to reach out and touch. Vibrant energy radiated off him the way heat did. He was a veritable vortex of pulsating anxiousness. Dangerous. Ferocious. Scary.

Kit didn't want to look at him. He wasn't the priority at the moment. Payback was. To hell with her beastly companion's thoughts on justice versus revenge. She was ready for a fight, primed for a final showdown with the fanged abomination that had stolen everything from her.

Night air became dense, as if it had been compressed by a giant's fist. Distant noise was drowned out by the sound of the werewolf's breathing.

Kit felt the atmosphere shift. An invisible door opened and closed in her expanding awareness, allowing an image to take shape. Fetid smells accompanied that hazy, wavering image. She recognized the odor as the smell of death.

The werewolf also scented the oncoming

presence. He shook his head, probably remembering the trio of fang-bearing freaks he had met earlier. But this was far worse, Kit needed to tell him. This was a really bad thing. Death incarnate. Evil itself.

She said nothing like that to the wolf, though. All of her attention was focused on the thing melting in and out of the darkness covering the street—a slithering form that threw no shadow as it passed beneath glow of the solitary street light.

Kit heard that beast's rustle, felt its imminent arrival, and she geared up to meet it with her blood pounding in her ears. Beside her, standing tall, the werewolf was quiet. The scope of his energy made her dizzy.

Though she was strong, angry, and as fierce as anything on the planet could have been, Kit appreciated the wolf's closeness. But though her werewolf companion was large, fast, and hot-blooded, she wasn't sure if those things would prove good enough to challenge something as completely and utterly dark as this other vampire was.

And yet, God… how she loved this wolf for his willingness to try.

*

Jared's special sight picked up movement down the block. His growl welcoming that beast was like a storm sifting through gravel.

The vampire in the distance came on, sliding closer and closer in the shadows, seemingly unconcerned about the welcoming committee. The female next to him who carried a grudge for the oncoming freak didn't so much as twitch a muscle. Contrary to his own anxiousness, she was like a black hole of motionlessness—a deep, dark hole, waiting for someone to fall in.

Her pale face was set. Her lips were parted so that only the points of her fangs were visible. Against her colorless skin, those fangs gleamed with a paler kind of luminosity.

The air around them began to thicken as the distant streetlight sputtered out. Only the moon cast shadows now, but the abomination they waited for was easier to see in the moon's silvery light.

It wore clothes that rippled, and moved on eerily silent feet. Slowly, Jared began to perceive its shape, which would have been freakishly large when this bloodsucker had been human and alive. But its size was no match for a werewolf whose wildness had blossomed beneath a full moon. A werewolf with a ferocious need to protect the female beside him.

He heard her mutter, "Come on, you filthy bastard. See what you've done."

For an instant, Jared pondered what sort of image they presented standing there—a wolf and vampire on the same team, hoping to confront the bad guys. But thoughts were a luxury there was no time to pursue. In a further slip of dark-on-dark, the beastly brute of a vampire arrived.

Jared stiffened when the thing faced them. Small shocks of revulsion ran through his system. This bloodsucker was similar in appearance to the freaks he'd seen earlier, while giving off a deadlier vibe.

The female beside him had faced this sucker and lost her life.

Inside Jared, his wolf whined and twisted at its leash as if recognizing an old enemy. In response, Jared raised both hands to display his claws, and let another growl rip.

The vampire couldn't be described in detail. The harder Jared looked, the less he saw of the sucker's face. The thing across from him seemed to move, even in stillness, so that its shape remained blurry. Though it hadn't taken a final step, Jared felt as though the creature was breathing down his neck. The sensation was extraordinarily chilling.

This bloodsucker was male, or had been once-upon-a-time. What was left of any former life had been burned away by time and the kind of massive intent to do harm that twisted nature. Jared felt this twist. Seeing the cadaverous creature was a startling revelation about how many things actually existed in state of pure evil without anyone, except its victims, noticing.

If this thing had a voice, it didn't use one. If it stared back, Jared couldn't find its eyes. Images flashed through Jared's mind about the little vamp next to him and her encounter with this hellish beast. What other possible outcome could there have been for a young woman accosted by one of the devil's minions, other than the result that had taken place?

Christ, maybe this was the devil.

"You dare to return here?" his feisty vampire companion called out in a voice that was steady, for all her obvious anxiousness.

There was no response from the abomination. Then again, Jared hadn't really expected one. The creature seemed to glide sideways, moving to the right and back in Jared's field of vision as if it never remained in one spot for long. Its shape stretched, shrank, stretched again without settling on any one definable size.

Yeah. Totally creepy.

Repulsed, Jared widened his stance. The female beside him strode ahead, daring to get closer to the dark, edgeless blur. She had things to say.

"I know you. There's no way anyone could forget such a monster. How many more of us have you made in the time that has passed? How many souls have you sentenced to Purgatory merely to feed your insatiable thirst?"

Jared knew the time for questions was over before the fanged abomination lunged for the beautiful victim whose soul that sucker had missed the first time around.

It took Jared fewer than three seconds to respond to that threat.

Chapter

SEVEN

Kit met the vampire with rage.

The nasty beast stank of the bloody dinner it had recently ingested. Up close, the monster looked much worse than it smelled.

There was no time for her to be sorry the werewolf had to see this, and what she could become when she undertook full vamp mode. But having already seen her fangs, the wolf had to understand the situation better.

Kit charged forward with a speed she had been practicing and had mastered for just such an occasion as this one. The final showdown. Only now, in the corner of her soul that had mistakenly been left to her, she pined for life. Where she had only yesterday been ready and willing to end it all, Kit now had succumbed to other feelings. Leftover human feelings.

Meeting the wolf had changed things.

But it was too damn late to veer off-course.

She met her nemesis with force, in a clash of bodies that would have shattered living bone. She wasn't alone. The werewolf was there, too, reaching past her to snag the dark creature's ragged coat with his claws.

Tugging hard, her wolf managed to spin the creature to the side, separating her from the freak for the few precious seconds it took for Kit to execute a jump. Landing hard on the creature's shoulders, Kit issued a throaty war cry that rang loudly in the night before she rested her mouth on the death-dealer's bony neck.

She bit down on a spot beneath the creature's left ear. Her fangs sliced deeply through the leathery, fetid-smelling flesh. Black blood spurted from the wound like dark liquid emerging from an oil-rig, but the wound quickly sealed over. The monster flailed its arms in an attempt to brush her off, realizing that the werewolf facing him was a bigger issue to deal with.

As the wolf battered the beast, Kit bit down on the nasty flesh again and again, over and over, stabbing with her teeth in several locations in search of a vulnerable spot that might weaken a demon that seemed far too strong. Each bite brought back memories of the night she had first encountered this creature, and how hard she had fought him that time, too. But this was different. This time, she was ready, and had some strength of her own.

The werewolf fought like a madman, punching, spinning, ducking to maintain his hold on the creature that roared with another startling cry of anger. They whirled in a macabre dance of give and take, but the wolf made sure the monster's snapping jaws couldn't reach his neck.

Kit's magnificent wolf was fast on his feet and used his strength like a prizefighter. Each movement was astonishingly graceful. And though the vampire lunged and its yellow-tinted canines came close enough to the wolf's bare chest to draw blood, those fangs found no purchase.

Kit wanted to shout every obscenity she knew, uncertain about how long this fight might go on, and whether her beautiful werewolf would tire before the vampire did. She hated to imagine what might happen then.

As she attacked with her teeth, she was sorry she had involved the wolf and could have kicked herself for calling him back here. If he were to be hurt, she'd be alone again, and didn't think she could stand that. Not after meeting him. *Not after this.*

Both of her hands closed around the vampire's neck. Using all of her considerable strength, Kit squeezed until the vampire slowed its moves slightly. And then Kit found herself on her feet, on the pavement in a crouch, having been flung there with one good shake.

Her hands were on the ground, and no longer on the vampire's neck, because the vampire was gone. It had vanished.

The werewolf was staring at his empty hands as if he wasn't quite sure what had happened. His questioning gaze then moved to her.

"I don't think we made a dent," Kit said as she straightened up.

She was covered in black blood and smelled like hell warmed over. The stench would have sickened anyone within ten feet of where she and the werewolf stood. It had to sicken the wolf.

Unable to speak without proper human vocal chords, the werewolf raised his face to the moon and howled. As the harrowing sound careened through the empty street, he moved toward her.

For the second time that night, Kit let him trespass in her personal space. She could have run away, left him there, slunk into the dark places where she'd regroup and wait to fight another day. She could have disappeared. Let the werewolf go. This was her fight. He had done enough.

She was in his arms before the idea about hitting the road found any real merit, and being swept off her feet. After that, they were running. He was running. She was merely a passenger, and as unlikely a damsel in distress as anyone could have conceived of.

Her wolf had something in mind for this strangely erotic charade of strong-man-carries-weak-female-to-safety, and for the moment, damn her vampire hide, Kit was intent, if not exactly content, to play along and see where this might lead.

At the very least, she'd see to it that the wolf got home safely before she hustled back to find out if that fanged demon would reappear for round two.

*

Jared understood that the female in his arms was allowing him the leeway to act as her protector. Hell, she had fought that dark beast like nothing he had ever seen.

In the back of his mind lay the idea that she could at any time turn right around and use that same strength of purpose, as well as her fangs, on him. He just refused to believe she would. For the moment, he wanted to comfort her in some small way and show her that monsters like the one they had just confronted were as unacceptable to him as they were to her, no matter their species. She would believe that because he had already told her about his own bad night on that blasted street.

Jared supposed they were both in a kind of post-battle limbo that had left them silent and scarred. But he had a lot to consider.

Traveling through an overpopulated city in werewolf form was always close to impossible, but due to the hour, luck was on his side on this weeknight. After all these months, Jared knew the route well, and the female in his arms was no burden at all. She weighed next to nothing, as if her bones and muscles were composed of imagery and contained no real mass. Vampire or not, Jared liked holding her. He had started to think of her as a woman, and nothing more.

So he ran, keeping to the darker places when necessary and sprinting through the open when the way was clear. His bundle of dangling arms and legs said nothing. Not one word. She could have made him set her down. She could have put a halt to this rescue by bearing her fangs. Instead, she stared up at him with a steady gaze that never faltered.

Big dark eyes zeroed in on his face as if she would soak up and memorize every detail. And while her slender body was cool to the touch, her laser-like scrutiny was extremely hot. The unabashed staring routine made Jared's body temp soar.

Slowing when they reached his apartment building, Jared took a good look around. No one was in sight. He glanced up at his balcony.

His vampire spoke at last. "Better change back, unless you can climb up the outside."

Jared waited out several more heartbeats while he weighed his options. If he set the vampire down, would she vanish like the monster they had fought? If she did disappear, he'd have to wait to hear more of her story. He would have to hunt her down.

He had fought by her side, on her side, and didn't even know her name. And after seeing the creature she faced, Jared's heart had broken in the little vampire's honor.

When she wriggled, Jared finally set her on her feet. He couldn't keep her there against her will and he was smart enough know that bringing her to his home had been as much a selfish act as for her protection. She was unearthly beautiful, interesting, strong. The darkness of their plights had increased their bond.

"What do you expect to happen next?" she asked, facing him, pushing back her hood.

Light brown hair fell across her shoulders like another blood spill, straight and untrimmed. It softened her angular face and made her skin look paler. Jared's body reacted with the slightest pulse of appreciation for her looks.

He motioned for her to start climbing, and took

hold of the brick. Without waiting to see if she'd follow, he climbed to his balcony and over the iron railing, and breathed a sigh of relief when his boots touched the tile.

Turning around, he found her crouched behind him, perched on the railing as if she were a bird able to cling to the narrowest of surfaces. She watched him closely as his reverse shift began, never taking her eyes off him.

"It's okay," he said breathlessly when his voice returned. "You can be safe here for a while."

"Safe from whom?" she returned.

She had him there. She hadn't been afraid of the monster they'd met, but maybe she had concerns about her current companion. Possibly she had felt the way his body hardened when he carried her, and now wondered about him being the newest version of predator.

"You're welcome to stay out here if that will make you feel better," he suggested. "But in all honesty, you smell like hell and could use a rinse."

"In your shower?"

"My bathroom is at your disposal."

She tilted her head. "Why aren't you afraid of me?"

"I might ask the same thing of you, but then we'd be going around in circles, wouldn't we? We are what we are."

A smile appeared on her face that made her seem younger. She said, "You feel sorry for me."

Jared nodded. "I suppose that's true."

"That makes me nothing more than a sympathy case. A project for you."

"You're wrong. I feel your pain because I went through something grossly similar, but aside from that, I like you."

The vampire on his railing fell silent. Then she jumped down from the railing to stand beside him on the balcony.

"I'll stay out here if you'd prefer me to keep my distance," Jared said. "The bathroom is through that door and to the right. If you go left, you'll find clean clothes in the closet and in drawers."

She said, "Your clothes?"

Jared nodded.

"You'll invite a vampire in?" she asked.

He shrugged. "Tell me the movies didn't get all the details right and once I issue the invitation you can come back and try to bite me anytime you want to."

She smiled again, showing a hint of the tips of her fangs. "Sorry. Actually, we can come and go as we please without invitation. I did mention, however, that werewolves don't taste very good?"

"So you won't be haunting me, then?"

Her dark eyes were again on his. "That depends."

"On what?"

"This," she muttered, pressing herself to him and looking up to check his reaction. "And whether you can forget our differences long enough to take that shower with me."

In a night full of surprises, Jared thought this last one was over-the-top.

C h a p t e r

EIGHT

Kit could have laughed at the wolf's reaction to her suggestion if she actually remembered how to laugh. She had existed for so long in a somber state, the emotion rising up tickled her throat until she let the laughter out.

And it felt good.

It felt as though some color had been added back into her black and white world, and as if her heart, long dormant, had been jump-started.

Yet she had to be careful about those feelings. She couldn't afford to go soft and forget her goal about dealing that hellish vampire a final death blow. Any relationship with an outsider now, however slight or temporary, might steer her in another direction.

Her shower challenge surprised the wolf and rendered him speechless for so long, Kit dug up another short bark of laughter.

The wolf said, "You find this funny, do you?" But he smiled that enticing smile Kit had loved since the first time she'd seen one like it, further lightening the mood.

"Not funny at all," Kit replied. "I'm deadly serious."

His smile widened as he rolled with her play on words.

"The sun will rise soon," he said. "What will happen then?"

"I will sleep."

"In a…"

The word *coffin* went unsaid.

Kit shook her head. "Preferably in your bed."

The way the wolf briefly closed his eyes told her he had wanted this, and also let her know that he wouldn't have asked.

His smile remained fixed as he said, "What's your name?"

"Names have power," she returned.

"So does anonymity."

"Kit. I'm Kit."

The wolf nodded. "I'm Jared."

Kit stepped back far enough to lose some of his heat. "I sort of prefer calling you *wolf*. To the right, you said? Hot water and towels?"

"Yes. To the right," the wolf who now had a name confirmed.

Kit liked the fact that this guy was strong and different. She longed to touch him, smell him, dwell within his warmth for the time being. After that, she would go. She'd leave Jared the wolf and return to her former existence, bolstered by the knowledge that kindness still existed in a world that grew colder by the day.

She went through the glass doors and into the wolf's lair, aware of his lingering gaze. He was trying to decide if she had been serious, and therefore wasn't eager to make a move.

Pausing in the middle of just the kind of large, airy room she had pictured as his living space, Kit said over her shoulder, "Your apartment is big. Maybe you'd better show me the way."

When he walked toward her, Kit turned her head so the wolf wouldn't see her determination to have something of her former life returned to her in this way. And also so that she wouldn't give away her anticipation for what might happen next.

He passed her with a light brush of his hand on hers that made Kit's shoulders twitch. This was all so bloody normal, or would have been for human beings about to have a date with a mattress. But she wasn't normal. Could never be normal. The wolf would blend with the rest of the world most of the time, while she'd cling to the dark.

She caught up with him in a long hallway. Sensing her sudden closeness, the wolf stopped walking. He didn't turn around. Kit heard his heart racing.

"It really is okay," he said. "Don't think you owe me anything for having your back out there. I don't like the word *pretend*. My life is all about pretending and I get enough of that on a daily basis."

"I never do anything I don't want to do," Kit said. "Remember that."

When he turned to face her, the force of her full frontal attack knocked the wolf backward and into a wall. Seconds later, her fangs were feathering over his lower lip and she heard his surprised intake of breath.

"I can be dangerous," she whispered. "This can be dangerous."

He said, "So can crossing a street."

"Not quite the same," Kit pointed out.

"I'll take my chances."

Kit took his lip between her teeth and bit down lightly. Then she waited to see what he would do.

She didn't have to wait long.

The wolf spun her around, reversing their places, trapping her between the wall and his rock-hard body. He spoke again with his mouth hovering over hers. "If you bite me, I'll bite back."

Kit said, "Is that a promise?"

Even more promising was the hardness between his thighs—proof of the very real seriousness of his interest in her. Noting the truth of that, Kit closed her eyes, suddenly comfortable with being trapped like this in the wolf's home. Comfortable with him.

He rested his lips on hers, not giving a damn about her fangs. Then he gradually increased the pressure of the kiss.

It was the first real meeting of their bodies in a situation where no other contact counted. Kit found the kiss sensual, sexy, and erotic. The wolf's breath in her mouth and in her lungs kicked up more distant memories that made her reach for him. A year ago, she had breathed. She had held down a job in a bookstore and had afforded a small apartment. Though she'd been orphaned early on, she'd had plenty of friends and hadn't wanted for much.

All those things came back to her in the wolf's warm breath.

All that in one brief kiss.

She kissed him back with fervor and fierceness that he matched move for glorious move. The kiss quickly became a devouring, a deep, drowning thing without beginning or end. Kit demanded more warmth, more of the wolf's blistering heat that was so evident in his talented mouth. Hunger for him was overpowering.

His hands went to her thighs and slipped underneath them. He lifted her up. Kit wrapped her long legs around him. Her grip was tight. Like this, she was centered over the stiff male body part tucked inside the wolf's jeans. Through her pants and his, Kit felt how physically attuned he was to the green light she was giving him. The only question now was how long it would take them to reach the heights of what they both wanted. Two species merging—one with fangs, the other with fur.

How could anything good possibly come of that?

And when the wolf did the unthinkable, withdrawing his mouth, sliding his lips down her cheek and toward her neck, Kit waited in desperate anticipation. When he nuzzled a spot beneath her ear, then took her skin between his teeth and bit down the way lovers sometimes did, the way wolves in the wild showed affection for their mates, she came unglued.

Throwing her head back, Kit hit the wall hard but tightened her hold on the wolf's incredible body. She snaked her hands over his taut buttocks in an attempt to pull him closer, but of course that was absurd, since there was no space separating them. He took no breath without Kit feeling the way his chest expanded. He was warm all over.

There were too many clothes in the way.

Too damn many clothes.

Gathering her strength, Kit pushed off the wall. They stumbled backward until they stood in the center of the hallway, teetering on the wolf's heels. His face was close to hers. He eyed her with a bright blue gleam.

"First," he managed to say. "First, we have to get rid of that bastard's blood."

Kit clung to him like some kind of living vine, legs wrapped around his waist, arms tightly around his neck, as her wolf headed for step two in whatever kind of relationship they were going to have tonight.

*

Jared was reluctant to separate himself from the female he intended to love to within an inch of the spirit of her former life. So he turned on the water in the shower and kicked off his boots. Fully clothed, he took her inside the shower stall, where hot water rained down.

When she made a sound that was a groan of pleasure, Jared echoed it with one of his own. And then their hungry mouths were pressed together again. The world became fuzzy after that. She was all that mattered. The woman in his arms didn't lack feminine whiles. Her hands, fingers, palms stroked his bare back beneath his coat, sending shivers of pleasure up his spine. She knew how to do just the right thing to enhance these moments. He couldn't have been more turned on.

But he had to push her away to get her naked. He also had to strip, and regretted having to change anything about moments that were mind-blowingly exotic and almost cruel by their very nature. What if he liked this too much? What if she didn't?

What could possibly compare to this if their future was to part ways?

The only light in the bathroom came from the main living space and bounced down the hallway. In the dimness, Jared's wolf vision served him well. He tore off her jacket and heard it hit the floor. She went for his coat. Water pasted her shirt to her body, but they were too wrapped up in each other for Jared to see much more of her shape.

Her fingers roamed over him, touching, scratching, at times digging in when their kisses grew still more intense. All of this added to the extremes of the pleasure being served up.

When she drew back, Jared spun around, letting the water spill over her hair, her face, her back. Her eyes were closed. Sighs of delight slipped from her half-closed lips—full lips that impossibly showed no signs of bruising from the obscene intensity of their kisses.

Black, foul-smelling monster blood dripped from her chest and flowed down the drain. Jared saw her better now—her breasts and her narrow chest. Her ribs stood out. Like the rest of her, Kit's flat, slightly concave belly was parchment white.

He wouldn't be able to feed her and fatten her up

because vampires didn't eat. Couldn't eat. Vampires were ruled by thirst. Would he approve of the way she managed that?

Acknowledgment of those facts didn't hamper Jared's passion. He hungered for her and her alone. Her vampire status was merely a minor setback.

Hell, was she mesmerizing him?

Making him want her so badly?

So be it.

When he turned off the water, she opened her eyes. But she didn't protest. In seconds, her shirt was with her jacket on the floor. Jared kissed his way down her stomach and tore open her pants. Supporting her body with one arm, he helped her out of those pants, then out of her wet boots.

Waiting for anything more than that was beyond him. Taking her pale long-fingered hand in his, Jared led her from the bathroom and back down the hallway, unconcerned about trailing water across the wood floor.

His bedroom was dark. The blinds were still closed and the bed was unmade. Jared led them straight to that bed without turning on a light. His companion would prefer the dark. She was used to the dark.

So be it...

She was on her back, on the bed, having slipped there fluidly. Jared went for his jeans, then stood beside the bed, open to her inspection in all his entire DNA-tweaked, human-like glory.

"Now," she said. Just that. *Now.*

He was weighted by muscle and she was so very

slim, but he couldn't hurt a vampire whose spine was backed by steel. Her invitation had told him so.

More foreplay wasn't in the cards. He was hard and aching, and her slim legs were open. She was waiting. She was willing. She wanted this.

The moment was crazy.

Jared rolled slowly onto the bed beside her, though it seemed she wasn't up for waiting to see what came next. In a flash of vamp speed, Jared was on his back and she was on top of him, on her knees, sliding over him, taking his hard length into her body.

The sound that came from him was a mixture of pleasure and surprise. Kit was cool inside, and plush. Her body was pliant, flexible, eager. The way her body swallowed him whole was another surprise. Though he sank deeply into her, she was in charge. When he was fully buried inside her exotic depths, she began to move her hips—not with gentle rocking motions, but with a series of sharp attacks.

His little vampire rode him as if seeking something that lay beyond her grasp; as if to convince herself that she could still feel alive in some small way. Her actions made Jared want to shout. He wanted desperately to regain control of his body and hers, slow this down, take more time. But her pull on him was spectacularly strong.

He began thrusting his hips, rising to meet each slap of her body to his. He had reached his lover's core several times over and yet she wanted more. She seemed to need more.

All right.

Okay, my little beast.

If that's what you need.

He gave her everything, with his hands on her hips and his cock hitting true. And when he felt her start to stiffen, he became aware of the rise of a distant drum beat inside her… beating faster and faster, coming closer, carrying him along before rapidly overtaking him with the fury of a whirlwind.

Suddenly, her movement ceased. She went rigid in his hands. And when the orgasm she had been searching for arrived, his lover screamed. Half shout, half cry, the sound she made seemed to go on and on.

Jared had closed his eyes. It took time for him to come down from the high he had just experienced, and he feared he might have died in the process. It took a blast of cool air on his chest to make him look up. His lover's weight had been lifted from him, and he wanted it back. He glanced sideways to find her, ready to gather her tight, prepping for a rematch.

But she wasn't beside him. She wasn't on the bed. Jared sat up, feeling bad about this. There was no hint of her in the room. He couldn't hear her in the hallway. Had what they had done been too much for the little lost soul?

Goddamn it. She was gone.

And he just wasn't ready to let her go.

Chapter

NINE

Kit ran like the wind on bare feet, wet, naked, scared.

She had experienced the sublime when she had believed that kind of pleasure to be behind her, buried in another lifetime. She had felt an emotion that was curiously, suspiciously, like love, and that too was awkward to contemplate. She had fangs, for Christ's sake. She was no longer a living, breathing woman. The things she had done since becoming a vampire would have kept her from the pearly gates even if she had been issued a get-out-of-hell-free card.

And now this.

Him.

Jared, her incredible werewolf, was a big reminder of all the good things she was missing. Still, there was no way a liaison like theirs would be allowed to stick. So what if she wanted him badly? All good things were taken away eventually. If their passionate meetings were to continue, Jared would eventually end things because what did she have to offer? Seeing no future, no chance of having a family, and without being able to see her in the daylight or introduce her to his friends, what did that leave for him?

Nothing.

The werewolf would go away, and that was as it should be. Jared was human-like most of the time. He he deserved better. He deserved more.

Bumping up her speed, Kit ran faster, trying to outdistance her feelings for what had just transpired in his apartment. Sunrise sat on the horizon, somewhere east of the city. Beyond the buildings she raced past was a healthy pink glow that warned her to take cover. Believing she could beat the system had been a failed early lesson. Vamps burned in the sunlight. Their skin turned black and crispy.

Kit wiped away the tears stinging her eyes, determined to go back to the way things were before she had met Jared. She was fine on her own, without anyone. She had made do for a year while waiting for the evil fanged monster to return to the scene of its crime. One of its crimes, anyway.

She was tired of being a victim. For a little while, the wolf had changed things, but she had to move on and forget him. She had to try.

Sliding around a corner as the sky's pink glow became yellow and the air brightened, Kit found her dark place very near to the alley where she and the wolf had fought the fanged monster. The basement room was in an old garment building, and well beneath ground level. She had long ago become accustomed to the smell of mildew and mice, and was used to total darkness underground. This was a safe place. She could rest and dream of the werewolf. She supposed he would occupy her thoughts and dreams from now on. By now, he'd be tucked into his comfortable bed without her.

"Will you dream about me, wolf?"

The door closed behind her, and Kit threw the bolt. Her bed wasn't nearly as soft as Jared's and didn't welcome her with enveloping warmth. The cold had returned, along with her anger for having allowed pent-up passion get the better of her.

"Tough shit showing weakness," Kit muttered as her eyelids began to droop. "Take what you can get, vampire, and deal."

As the enveloping blackness came and her mind began to shut down, Kit felt the wetness of one last tear slide down her cheek.

Because all of the protests were lies, and she knew it.

*

Although Jared eventually dropped off to sleep, he didn't dream. He got up a few hours after sunup telling himself he could have imagined everything… until he found *her* clothes on the bathroom floor.

Not his imagination, then. Kit had been here.

He felt a flash of heat at the thought. What they had done in his bed had been spectacularly wicked, due to his little vampire's incredibly talented, provocative mastery of the fine art of pleasuring a werewolf. Thinking about how she had learned those kinds of tricks wasn't in his best interest, and yet the desire for a replay was already making him hard. Then there was the idea of her running around the city naked.

She had a name. Kit.

He liked to think it. Say it.

However, any attempt to find her again would have to wait. Though he'd count each tick of the clock, wishing he could hurry things along, there were far too many hours until the next sundown.

Where had she gone?

No doubt she would have nested somewhere near the street where they had met. Jared was sure of that. The first rule in assessing an enemy was to become familiar with the area that enemy used, and learn all of its secrets. Kit had been going to that same place for a long time. She had admitted to observing him month after month. She would be near there. Someplace close by.

Kit the vampire.

Jared shook his head, wondering if her nemesis would return after nightfall. Having been bested, would that monster stage a comeback? Could Jared James help her again when the full moon phase had passed, leaving him with just one last harder-than-usual shape-shift until the arrival of next full moon?

Leftover cell turnover would allow him that last shift if the moonlight was still strong—which meant that if he went back to that street tonight, it would be in human form, and for as long as possible before letting the wolf out. If a fight became necessary, he'd be weaker than usual, but still a hell of a lot stronger than most of the people and creatures he might encounter. If Kit's monster reappeared, a werewolf without the moon's push toward full strength would be at a slight disadvantage, and yet he was willing to work with what he had.

And if his own monster-maker were to show up, he'd meet that challenge as well.

In his mind, Jared's kept going over the possibilities of what might happen when he and Kit met again. His body liked the idea. Hell, it was hard to think of anything else when he smelled her on his skin and on his sheets. The unique fragrance of night scents lingered all over his apartment, concentrated mostly in the clothes she had left behind.

Kit had been in a hurry to get away.

Why?

"Can you feel me thinking about you, Kit? Do thoughts of me, and what we did together disturb your slumber the way you've again disturbed mine?"

No immediate sense of her came to him, and Jared lamented that fact. Finding her became an absolute necessity. He couldn't have imagined that a vampire could be so sexy and sensual, or that she would have so quickly cast a spell to ensnare him. Yet that's exactly what Kit had done. She had cast a spell.

Holding her damp jacket, Jared scanned the parts of the city he could see from his balcony. Soon, people would start moving about. Already, there were cars in long morning parades, and sirens in the distance. Last night's fight with the ruffians and the old vampire made him anxious to rejoin the police force. Help was needed in this city. He was stronger than ever and could work things out with his wolf if he went back to work.

But first, he had to find Kit.

Breakfast was short and tasteless when he remembered that Kit couldn't eat. The shower seemed empty without her. Yes, he was acting like a lovesick fool, but couldn't help it. Maybe helping Kit with her plight would end this sudden solitary torture. Maybe they would meet both monsters-makers and even the score. After that, and with nothing more in common, he and Kit would go their separate ways somewhat appeased. No sharing a bed. No hot seduction of the senses. Absolutely no sex.

"Maybe."

And maybe not.

Who was he kidding?

She was a good, if unusual, match for a werewolf. Rough stuff couldn't hurt her. She couldn't catch whatever he had. Kit wasn't just anybody, she was wily, strong and also had things to hide.

"Possibly not a match made in heaven," Jared muttered. "But good enough for now."

In the cool breeze that met him, he imagined Kit laughing over that kind of sentiment. And he smiled.

*

The cold was numbing. Kit had always wondered about that, and about her ability to feel anything at all. Yet her body felt exceptionally chilled after having experienced the werewolf's molten heat. Jared's heat. In his apartment. His bedroom.

The memory of those hours made this next night seem like winter. And by the way, she was missing her favorite clothes.

There was no way she'd go back to Jared's apartment and get them. Hell is where she had landed—back here on the street, looping over and over in the same scene, the same scenario, waiting for an end to the nightmare she had been part of for the past year. If she were being honest, she had to admit that meeting Jared face-to-face and groin-to-groin had made things worse for both of them.

Where before she had only one objective, single-mindedly pursuing that goal, her thoughts now kept straying to another creature instead of the one she sought. The hot one. The one who had made her forget what she was for a few hours. The creature that had made her feel like a woman, and desirable.

Jared. Kit had woken with his name on her lips and she repeated that name again now, hoping he would come back, while at the same time hoping he wouldn't. Being near to the wolf complicated things. Thinking about him made the rest of the world seem vague.

She stood on the ledge above the street, waiting for something to happen, wishing the abomination that had savaged her would appear.

The night was quiet. Moonlight bounced off the asphalt. No clouds diluted the strength of that light. The distant streetlight hadn't been repaired, so there were shadows everywhere.

Too many shadows.

When the air shifted suddenly with a familiar weightiness, Kit turned her head. One jacketless shoulder twitched as she caught a whiff of a masculine scent. *His* scent.

Be careful what you wish for…

Jared appeared in the distance, walking toward her as if he owned the street. He was in human form, and always as formidable as the werewolf inside him. Kit felt the wall of heat his body gave off from where she stood. She had wished too hard for this moment instead of the one that had them going their separate ways. She had drawn a wolf to her in the bloodsucker's place.

Jared was dressed in jeans and a different black coat. His blue shirt was open at the neck, showing off far too much bronzed skin for Kit not to notice. Her wolf didn't say hello or offer mundane conversation when he stopped beneath the ledge and looked up. His eyes found hers, and that was that.

"Round two?" he said in a tone that though hoarse, was also like velvet to someone unused to comfort.

Kit didn't make any attempt to come up with a testy comeback.

"Do you think that thing will return tonight?" he asked when she failed to fill the silence, though Kit knew he wanted to say something more personal.

"Yes," she finally replied. "The beast will be angry and wanting payback."

"Good. I'm in the mood for delivering some good old-fashioned justice."

"It's not your fight, wolf."

"Jared," he reminded her. "And as I've told you, protecting the streets is what I do."

"You're making it personal because of me," Kit pointed out.

His eyes never wavered. His gaze, on her, was disconcertingly intense. There was a new light in his eyes, and a new set to his jaw… and all of that made him more attractive. Kit wanted to jump his bones. She could hardly hold back. Inside her, she ached for him and for what he had to offer. This is what having a soul did. What *he* had caused without knowing it. She should have hated Jared for that, and instead…

Instead…

Kit closed her eyes to deal with the emotion welling up.

The wolf spoke softly. "I believe my need to help you is personal. Aside from last night and what took place in my apartment, I feel as though we're connected in some way. Maybe we met before your date with a dark fate. Could that be why I can't get you out of my mind? You're part of my former life?"

How much can I tell you, wolf?

What will you think?

After all, I would have been like them if you hadn't showed up—just a mindless thing with no ties to my past and no conscience. I might have been one of the bloodsuckers you're now set to fight.

"I'm right," he said, reading into her blank expression. "We have crossed paths before."

"Yes," Kit admitted. "Only slightly. Never up close."

"Thank heavens for that," he said. "And for the fact that I'm not going mad. Tell me about it."

"It's a story for another time."

"Because we have so little time here tonight?" the wolf taunted.

"Because that same wicked fate you spoke of might again be playing tricks and we're the poor suckers on the receiving end."

When the wolf's blue eyes widened at the vehemence in her tone, Kit was sorry she had said those things out loud.

"So, we had a bad connection," the wolf said. "It had to be slight, however, because I would have remembered you."

"Very slight," Kit agreed, ignoring the pleasure of his offhanded compliment.

The wolf tore his gaze from her long enough to glance around at the street. "Did we meet here, by any chance?"

"Why do you think that?" Kit countered.

"Because it seems quite a coincidence that we're both here, and that we feel a connection to each other and to this place."

Smart didn't even begin to describe this guy and his infernal insight, which made Kit contemplate her next move carefully. She decided to tell him something; enough to satisfy his curiosity. Nodding, she said, "We met in passing here."

"But you recognized me?" he pressed.

"Yes. You also, it seems, are hard to forget."

The blue gaze continued to probe. "Did you see what happened to me here?"

"No," she was quick to reply.

His next question struck true and rattled her confidence about withholding pertinent information. "Was I here when you met with your fate?"

Dilemma. If she said yes, she would have to fill

Jared in on the rest of the story. Saying no would be a lie, and maybe even a disservice. In any case, neither of them owed the other anything really. Their night in the sack had been blissful, but everyone would agree there was no future in prolonging the pain of two beings from two different species' comingling on a more permanent basis.

Get it over with, Kit's conscience nagged. *Tell him what part he played in my new existence.*

"You were close by when I lost my life, and came running," she said.

The wolf looked surprised.

"You didn't find me," Kit added. "The bloodsucker had dragged me to the rear of the alley with his fangs in my neck."

"No," Jared, her wolf, protested. His voice was hushed.

"Saving me wasn't in the cards," Kit continued. "Wasn't in anybody's cards."

He interrupted her. His focus grew even more intense. "You said you have a soul, and that it's unusual for a vampire to retain one. How did that happen?"

It was too late for games now, having gone this far. Jared felt their connection as keenly as she did and wanted an explanation for the bond.

Kit said, "The bloodsucker didn't finish what he had started. The beast didn't steal my soul or set it free—or whatever the hell they do to rid a person of their essence after they brutally die. My soul was mine to keep."

Again, the wolf said with some insight, "What

part did I play in that, Kit?"

Maintaining eye contact with Jared, she said, "Your presence sent the vampire away before he could take all of me."

There it was. The reason for their strange connection and why they were drawn to each other. Long ago, it had become obvious to Kit that her soul longed for its rescuer. But how much stock could be placed on the workings of a nebulous ball of spirit that no one had yet proved actually existed? What the hell was a soul, anyway?

"Was that a good thing?" Jared asked in a gentle voice that belied the power he possessed.

Kit had no answer for that question. She wasn't sure about anything after meeting Jared and falling for him. Did souls create attraction? Is that where the concept of love resided? Should she continue to curse that soul and Jared's part in leaving her with it when she had been hungering for this wolf since she had first seen him?

No matter what she had thought, or how much she had argued to the contrary, she now had to fully admit to herself that he was part of the reason she had hung around this street, all this time. No maybe. No getting around it.

Suddenly, Kit felt inept at dealing with the situation, and temporarily tongue-tied.

Jared said nothing more, but his eyes flashed brightly as the moonlight slid sideways, moving closer to his right shoulder. His fingers curled and uncurled. He rolled his broad shoulders before reluctantly dragging his attention from her and turning to look behind him.

For the past few seconds, Kit had known what was coming. Now, her lover also knew the beast had returned. The night had coughed up a visit from last night's monster, and this time Kit almost welcomed the diversion. Being a vampire was one thing. Being a vampire in love was turning out to be an unexpected new twist on torture that no one could have expected.

C h a p t e r

TEN

The night air stank with an odor Jared would have attributed to a pile of dead, decaying bodies. There was no way an old bloodsucker like the one they had encountered the night before wouldn't have been noticed by anyone with a decent sense of smell, so it was a good thing the street was deserted.

Death was this guy's calling card.

Kit was off the ledge and beside him before Jared turned back, and she was reaching for something tucked inside the back of her waistband. Jared hoped she was after some kind of magic weapon only vampires knew about, because the big sucker heading their way was visibly upset.

Last night the creature had glided in on a stiff breeze. Tonight it moved disjointedly, with a hitch in its stride. Jared had gotten in a few good punches the last time they'd met, but Kit's teeth had done real damage to this brute—as much damage as she could inflict, given the obvious age and large size of the bloodsucker. Kit, as a human woman, would have been toast in seconds, but there was no time for Jared to circle back to the terrible image of her lying in a pool of blood.

A growl, human but fierce, stuck in his throat. Jared tore off his coat and flung it aside. Widening his stance, he faced the dangerous bloodsucker and smiled.

"My fight," Kit declared, standing beside him, echoing her earlier refrain.

"Yeah. About that…" Jared returned without finishing the sentence.

The cadaverous, red-eyed vampire sprang off its bony legs to land at the curb, just three feet away from where Jared and Kit were standing. It made a disturbing gurgling sound, and bared its fangs.

"Pathetic," Jared said, holding his ground. "I would have thought you learned a lesson last night about trespassing where you're not wanted."

Maybe the creature didn't have a voice or the ability to speak. Possibly it was too angry to make sense of the rebuke. However Jared chose to look at it, the end result was the same as far as this werewolf was concerned. It was going to be the last fight this red-eyed abomination would see, and the world would be a better place because of it.

But a strange thing happened before he or Kit made a move. Out of the darkness down the block came a wolfish howl that iced the back of Jared's neck. His internal warning system jumped to red alert because a wolf had made that sound, and Jared hadn't made it. Hell, he only knew of one other werewolf in this city.

Stealing a glance at the sky, where a not quite full moon lit the street with an opalescent glow,

Jared's inner wolf clawed its way upward.

He stopped Kit from advancing on the bloodsucker by stepping in front of her. At the same time, the big vampire hobbled sideways as if Jared wasn't the only one present who hadn't liked that not-too-distant howl.

Kit wasn't to be corralled, though. In a blur of speed, she went for the creature that had made her what she now was, lunging at the big bloodsucker as though she knew the story about David and Goliath. The set of her face told Jared she wasn't going to let this opportunity to even an old score slip away a second time.

Jared was torn. He knew what else was coming, and what soon would show up. Was his own monster-maker returning to confront his progeny, or to prove that *evil* was its middle name? Jared figured he had five seconds at most to decide which creature to tackle first, and which abomination was going to prove itself the king of monsters here.

Pushing off the curb, Jared hit the vampire square in the chest. Momentum was on his side. In spite of the fact that Kit went after her nemesis with hands, feet, and fangs, Jared succeeded in moving the beast directly into the brightest spot on the street.

Moonlight found him.

One more shift.

Only one left in me.

That shape-shift was the only thing that would allow him and his little vampire a modicum of success against the bleakness of the odds facing them.

Keyword: *modicum.*

Realigning facets of his spine snapped with a noise like that of young tree limbs breaking. Jared's face began to burn as his skin stretched to accommodate sharper cheek bones and a tighter jaw. Shoulders widened, forcing joints, muscles, and ligaments to join the expansion. His chest heaved. Ribs cracked. Leg muscled thickened, pressing the limits of the seams on his old blue jeans. During this process, Jared had to reach for each breath.

He had never tried this kind of shape-shift, utilizing leftover moon-fried nerves and cells not quite ready to forget the more wolf-like shape of the night before. Although he had always known it was possible, Jared hadn't anticipated the added level of pain that doubled him over and threatened to bring up his lunch.

No time for this...

When he straightened up, it was almost too late. The big bad werewolf-maker was looking at him from close range with savage eyes that Jared remembered all too well.

*

Kit swung herself sideways, ducking the vampire's snapping jaws and striking out at the creature with both hands and every ounce of strength she possessed.

"Not quite up to this tonight?" she taunted, speaking through the gap in her own fangs. "Need more time to recover, do we?"

Taunting further incited the old vampire. The bloodsucker began to solidify, his movement slowing slightly.

"More of your own medicine, maybe?" Kit purred, shifting her position fast enough to dodge a blow.

She was fully aware of the fact that Jared had shape-shifted. After the initial blow he had dealt this vampire, the moonlight had aided his transformation. He'd have more strength, more power like this. Jared, in werewolf form, would have scared the pants off anyone unlucky enough to witness such a thing.

But he had hesitated, and Kit sensed his sudden uneasiness. After skirting more of the old vampire's antics, she saw the reason Jared and the bloodsucker had become distracted. Another werewolf had joined the party—an unwelcome one, by the looks of things.

Kit felt her wolf's anxiety over facing this new and unexpected guest. Jared was both anxious and excited. The night wind seemed to whirl around him as he stood with his gaze locked on the other wolf.

It was Jared's werewolf, Kit realized. *The* werewolf. The one her lover had been searching for. The creature that had put a wolf inside Jared.

Hell...

The battle was about to get bloody.

*

The fact that Jared could understand what the werewolf across from him was thinking came as another surprise. So did the surge of power Jared felt when he realized how much larger than that wolfish bastard he was.

Yet he wasn't going to stand for the nasty thoughts that werewolf had about getting rid of its earlier creation, or the sideways glances that creature gave Kit, who was currently fighting the old vampire like a maniac.

Had this werewolf come across vampires before? Its attention snapped to the bloodsucker. And then he was on top of the vampire in a burst of speed not unlike Kit had shown, and it became obvious to Jared that the creepy vampire was a better target for a mentally messed up werewolf in need of a fight.

Jared breathed a sigh of relief. His attention didn't have to be divided between going after that werewolf and helping Kit fend off the pasty-faced bloodsucker's fangs.

Kit seemed reluctant to let the two beasts go at each other, which would have meant severing her personal battle with the source of her nightmares. She continued to fight until Jared grabbed her by the waist and stepped back to watch the two examples of vastly different species battle it out, no love lost between them.

Kit kicked out and shouted obscenities, needing to hurt that vampire, but being much stronger, Jared held her tightly. Even in these distressing moments, when witnessing the terrible strength of the two creatures beside them, she felt good in his arms. She felt like sex on a soft bed, and reminded him of the possibilities of naked bodies in a shower.

He hoped with all his might that this would end well. For the first time in a long, seemingly endless year, Jared wanted to live, thrive, and to get to know Kit better. He wanted to know who she had been before her life-altering event, and explore a long list of the things she liked. He wasn't above praying for those things.

The fight in front of them was loud and dirty. Kit kept squirming, not ready to give up her sense of justice to the other werewolf. Jared soothed her with soft growls that were whispered assurances—as many as he could come up with—about letting the monsters take care of themselves, and about being with her when this was all over.

Werewolf blood covered the ground. There was a great hole in the vampire's face caused by a pair of fatally sharp claws. Neither beast seemed to notice the damage they had been dealt and as minutes passed, the fight grew fiercer. Jared wanted to take Kit away, but feared that neither of these bastards would be taken out permanently. There was a dire need inside him to witness the end, see the final result, even if he had to jump in to ensure its success.

With a death grip on Kit's left wrist, Jared climbed onto the ledge, high above the scene. After more seconds passed, she began to settle down. Her gaze moved from him to the fight and back as if they had been far removed from what was taking place, and as if the ledge exemplified the concept of safety… when in actuality they were far from being safe.

Jared held her against his body, feeling each shiver that passed through Kit. With his arms around her and her back against his chest, he willed his warmth to ease her shudders.

He knew he would have to change back to human shape so he could talk to her, and that giving up some of his power was a risk he had to take. Kit had to be made to understand that she wasn't alone and wouldn't be ever again if she agreed to what he would propose. A partnership. A collaboration of justice-seekers who had been touched by the supernatural. A monster-hunting team. A couple.

The sounds of his reverse shift quieted Kit. She didn't turn around. Nor did she run away. The stabbing pain of this reversal was worth it, Jared told himself as the breath was siphoned from his lungs. Kit was worth it.

When his voice returned, he whispered to her, "We can do this together. All or nothing. You and me."

The werewolf on the street howled with anger and fury. Blood spatter—red, thick—speckled the ledge, but that wolf had pummeled the vampire to the ground, where black vampire blood pooled on the asphalt.

The werewolf, skin torn to shreds, leaned over to grab the vampire, but hesitated a second too long. Fangs came up, snapping with a force that ripped open the Were's chest. The vampire shoved both of its bony hands inside that bloody opening. Kit made a sound of dismay as the vampire's hands emerged holding a bloody, pulpy lump that was the werewolf's heart. And the werewolf, with a stunned expression on its face, crumpled.

Freeing herself from Jared's arms, Kit jumped to the street, reaching for whatever she had hidden in her waistband. She came up with a sharp wooden stake. Not a mysterious secret vampire-fighting weapon; just a piece of smooth carved wood, pointed at one end. And that was all it took for her to deal her fanged nemesis, already severely wounded in battle, its final death blow.

No sound accompanied the vampire's demise. There was a silent explosion, and the bloodsucker disintegrated into a funnel of dark gray ash. Soon, nothing remained of the bastard except a foul-smelling rain of musty dust particles.

Kit stood there for a long time, looking down. She was processing the termination of this long-awaited event, and Jared gave her all the time she needed. For her, the hunt was over. It was the same for him. Still, witnessing the death of the monsters that had made them in their image didn't alter the fact that nothing could change what he and Kit were. There was no rewind button.

The next steps he took would be important, Jared knew, and would provide direction for them both if Kit agreed. Possibly what came next would be his reawakening, and hers. He decided that perhaps he had stumbled into the area a year ago in time to save Kit's soul because fate had wanted him to have a partner. Fate might have coughed up an unlikely one, but hell, she'd be undaunted by the werewolf thing. And Kit was a damn good lover.

The passing moments seemed anti-climactic. After the fight that had taken place, the silence was absolute. Kit didn't move for the longest time. It seemed to Jared as though she couldn't. So, it was up to him to try to remedy things from here on out, and he found that idea scarier than confronting the old bloodsucker.

What did he and his little vampire have in common? Well, more than anyone would have guessed. She had fangs. He had claws. They were vigilantes, looking out for others, making sure no one else suffered the way they had. Together, they had just given the wheels of justice a damned good turn.

"Come home," he said, getting right to those future plans he had formulated the moment he had opened his eyes in bed to find her gone.

Kit turned to face him.

"Blackout curtains we can manage. And blood banks. If there's anything else, you can make me a list."

She said nothing and chewed on her lower lip with the tips of her fangs. But her dark eyes grew softer as her gaze swept over his face.

"I'm going back to work as a detective," Jared said. "I'll take the night shift, and everyone on the force will be relieved by that request. We…"

He let the rest of that sentence dangle. Was it too much, too soon, that he was asking?

"We what?" Kit raised an eyebrow questioningly and took one step closer to him.

Jared cleared his throat. Gangsters and bad guys

had never so much as given him pause, and yet he was inept when facing a woman.

"We can make it work," he finally said. "For as long as we want to."

Kit's dark eyes reflected concern. "Do you know how long that might be for me?"

"You mean the whole immortal thing?"

"I suppose I'll never really know it that's truth or fiction until more time passes by. What if all that living forever business is a lie?"

Jared waited for her to finish her thought.

"I'm pretty sure having a soul might change things. I'm not exactly sure how, though. If I'm nothing like the other suckers I've met, maybe I'll age and we..."

Jared liked the sound of that last word, even if she hadn't completed the idea. Like him, she was thinking in terms of *we*.

"Maybe werewolves also have a life extension clause," Jared said.

"And if you don't?"

"We can address that when we need to."

"Ever the optimist?" Kit suggested.

Jared shrugged. "Unless, of course, I'm the only one here who thinks we make a good pair."

Gracefully, Kit leaned over to sweep her wooden stake off the ground. She held it up to the moonlight, and then looked to him.

"Your bed is more comfortable than mine," she said.

Jared's pulse beat hard against his neck. Was he nuts, or had she just agreed to his proposal?

"Plus," she continued, "You're as warm as a heater most of the time."

He smiled. "So, that's it? Warmth and comfort are the keys to a successful arrangement?"

She was beside him before he blinked, with her hands on his chest. "No, there is something else."

Her hand began to slide downward, over his ribs, across his abs, stopping at the waist of his jeans.

Jared's smile broadened. He was fairly sure he knew where she was going with this. When she smiled in return, the tips of her fangs gleamed.

"Werewolves don't taste good," he reminded her.

"The fangs are permanent." Her fingers slipped beneath the waistband. "Get used to it."

Her fingers were cool, but Jared didn't mention how, for a werewolf whose body temp ran to the extreme side of hot, a touch of coolness was a blessing. He didn't mention that because he had other plans for his mouth.

He reached for Kit, pulled her close, waited until she looked up at him before speaking the last few words he'd be able to get out.

"Last chance to refuse me, Kit."

"Are all werewolves this dense?" she fired back just before his mouth devoured hers, fangs and all.

With a dead monster at their feet, gray vampire ash falling like snow, and the moon shining brightly overhead, they were suddenly naked, lusting, and going at each other as if nothing, not even the wheels of justice, could ever separate them again. And Jared vowed nothing ever would.

In that moment, Jared remembered what being happy felt like. It felt like Kit. He was happy, hungry, ravenous, really… and suddenly, with Kit so tightly, lushly, wrapped around him, Jared finally embraced the animal he had become.

~ The End ~

About Linda . . .

Linda Thomas-Sundstrom is the author of paranormal romance and urban fantasy novels and novellas, both dark and light, for Harlequin Nocturne and GothicScapes, with more than 30 stories trespassing in the supernatural realm.

Immortals, Angels, and Werewolves take over Linda's imagination most of the time. For Nocturne, her Vampire Moons and Blood Knights series deal with sexy immortals on a mission, with titles like: *Golden Vampire, Guardian of the Night, Immortal Obsession, Immortal Redeemed, and Angel Unleashed...* plus novellas.

If you love Weres, check out Linda's Wolf Moons series for Nocturne, and the following titles: *Red Wolf, Wolf Trap, Wolf Born, Wolf Hunter, Seduced by the Moon, Half Wolf, Desert Wolf...* plus several wolfish novellas.

If Urban Fantasy is what you crave, with unusual settings and both dark and lighter challenges... try Linda's Dark vs Light series of novellas... with titles like: *Hot Holiday, and Trapped in Stone.*

All books and novellas are available at online retailers. Grab one, or grab them all!

See more on Linda's web site:
www.lindathomas-sundstrom.com
Visit Linda on Facebook:
www.facebook.com/LindaThomasSundstrom

Wolf, Interrupted

Jillian Stone

C h a p t e r

ONE

Ms. Elle Hathaway weeds the poison garden.

Elle traced the intricate curves of the skull and crossbones with her fingertip. The sign on the gate read: These plants can kill. Do not touch or eat any plant! Children must be accompanied at all times.

"Shall we face *Atropa Belladonna,* the beautiful but deadly nightshade?" Julian rubbed his hands together and made Igor eyes, a comical face that always made her laugh.

She barely cracked a smile.

"Come on, Elle—not even an eye roll?" her coworker teased.

She sighed. "Do I have to?"

She and Julian were scheduled to work the beds in the most dangerous section of Chelsea Physic Garden. It was a job she looked forward to in the way one might anticipate the latest *Insidious* movie, with a quiver of fear and a slightly elevated pulse rate.

She chewed her lip. "You know this garden makes me nervous."

"Good God, of course it does." Julian slouched against the gate. "I blame my boorish behavior on drinking decaf this morning...Elle?"

There was nothing Julian could do to bring her back. Time and space had shifted.

She was a child kneeling beside the paralyzed body of her father. Her mother's whimper as clear and heartbreaking in memory as it had been eleven years ago. Elle had watched helplessly as her mother wiped away the purplish foam bubbling at the edges of her husband's mouth.

A rare and unusual death, the coroner had scribbled in the inquest report. His conclusion read: Accidental poisoning. No malicious intent.

Elle was still in primary school, but even she knew better. As head gardener of the Anton Ogilvie estate, her father well knew the difference between wolfsbane and delphinium.

Julian whistled. "Earth to Elle…?"

She covered her lapse with a smile. "Sorry, I'm a bit muddle-brained today."

"No, I'm the thick-headed one." He eyed her more seriously. "You're looking doubly spooked this morning."

"That's because I am spooked."

"You saw something."

She hesitated before nodding. "In the Covent Garden Station last night."

Julian opened the gate and she pushed the wheelbarrow into the dreaded poison garden. "That's the second sighting in less than a week, Elle."

"I know." She grimaced. "Last night was definitely not the usual."

"One of those sightings?" he asked in a low voice. "The kind you see, but no one else does."

She swallowed. "Possibly, but I don't think so."

"Want to talk about it?" Julian trusted her second sight more than she did.

A botanist like herself, and a new fellow to the Chelsea Physic Garden, there was a kindness in Julian she'd been drawn to and they'd hit it off immediately. So much so, they were already making plans to one day open a natural apothecary together. He was also funny and smart, and newly married to a handsome man who adored him.

Elle pulled on long gloves and adjusted her goggles. "Maybe later."

She and Julian each took one side of a long bed of foxglove. Latin name: *Digitalis purpurea*. Early each spring, annuals were sown and perennials were mulched and weeded. In another month, tall spires covered in bell-shaped flowers would shoot skyward. An entire bed of elegant, pale purple soldiers was a breathtaking sight to see.

She dug into the loamy soil, turning over crusty patches, working in handfuls of compost, thinning the clumps so newly sprouted leaves could grow. A part of Elle secretly marveled over these poisonous plants. Murderous as well as lifesaving therapeutic elixirs were derived from their mysterious flowering stalks. She pulled off a few remaining dead leaves and loosened the soil carefully around the last few clusters.

Besides, mortality was rare from *Digitalis*.

Not so with the next bed of *Aconitum napellus*—prince of death—aka wolfsbane. Lethal to wolves and humans alike, even to the touch. The plant that

127

had killed her father.

Julian hit a stubborn patch of soil. "Toss over a hand rake, Elle."

She stood up and rummaged in the cart. "There you are—" As she reached for the pronged tool, she caught an inkling of movement. More of a blur, really.

The scariest sights happened in the corner of her eye. Fleeting shadows that flickered at the edge of her peripheral vision. Most often, she was a second too late to catch a glimpse of the underworld. But occasionally—startlingly—she spied a monster.

A tall man wearing a long coat stood in the middle of the culinary garden. He appeared to be lost, or looking for someone. Longish, unruly hair fell over an upturned collar. And he wore his man-scarf well.

Quite the romantic figure, as if he emerged from another time. The intriguing man approached a volunteer guide escorting a group of school children. Elle strained to hear the conversation.

Typical of mornings in the middle of March, a blustery wind swept off the Thames, crisp and cold. Elle shivered, and passed the hand rake to Julian.

"I believe he asked for Tom." He offered with a wink.

She adjusted her kneepads and returned to a large clump of unruly plants. Tom Wells was the director of Chelsea Physic Garden. A good-natured gentleman, who ruled over the three-hundred-year-old medicinal garden with a meticulous, obsessive-compulsive spirit that infected the entire staff.

Julian's grin turned devilish. "Tall, dark and

mysterious. Just your type, Elle."

She worked the soil deeper. "Are you referring to the fabulous bed head with the upturned collar?"

"Ms. Luella Hathaway?" The disembodied voice came from behind and above.

She checked in with Julian, whose fluttery eye roll signaled a silent alert: Hot-man-standing-right-behind-you.

She sat back on her heels. "I'm Elle, short for Luella."

"Detective Inspector Durant, CID."

She ignored the queasy, tingly feeling and dared to look up. Stern and masculine, with a somewhat dangerous air about him. She noted strong, even features and a lovely wide mouth.

"Sorry." She stood up. "You caught me in the middle of spring mulching." She hoped her apology came off as self-consciously cute and not too flirty. "I must look a fright." She pushed the goggles back on her head, and blew a lock of hair out of her face.

Stray strands fell back in her eyes.

"Please, don't let me disturb your work." His glance moved briefly to Julian. "I'm here about the mauling in the Underground last night. I'd like to discuss the report you gave to an officer at Ebury Square Station. Is there somewhere we might go to talk? I've a few questions that require privacy."

His accent was on the posh side for a detective.

Elle tossed the same errant lock of hair back. Covered in rubber gloves up to her elbows, she lifted both hands. "As you may have noticed, I'm dressed for the poison garden." Stubborn strands returned to obscure her vision.

The inspector reached out. "If you would…allow me." Gently, he swept the unruly wisps off her cheek, anchoring them behind her ear.

Never mind her too flirty worries. This encounter had suddenly become wonderfully awkward. "Thank you."

She started to look away, but got caught up in his completely unnerving gaze. Sapphire blue eyes flecked with silvery light. They were the most unusual blue eyes she'd ever seen—crystalline yet piercing.

She literally had to catch her breath. "Will this take long? I've got several beds to finish, as well as the glass house."

The inspector held out his card.

"Better not." Elle wiggled her fingers. "I've been rummaging about in wolfsbane." She shot a wink across the bed to Julian. "We may not look it, but we're both covered in noxious particulates."

"Perhaps I could return around tea time." The inspector's answer floated over plant beds from a distance away. The disembodied voice prickled up and down her spine.

Elle spun around.

A quick scan of the grounds found him standing more than twenty feet away. The oddest feeling welled up inside her and she gasped for breath. It was as if all the air had been sucked out of the garden. "There's a cafe at the north end of the property," she stammered. "It's never crowded in the late afternoon."

She checked in with Julian, who appeared pale and confused.

"Four o'clock in the cafe, Ms. Hathaway." The detective turned down a tree-lined path and disappeared behind a curtain of green lace.

Julian's voice brought her back. "A police report about a mauling in a tube station. What the hell is going on, Elle?"

"I hardly know where to begin." She sighed. "Did you see that?"

"See what?" Julian had returned to weeding.

"One second he was here…and the next…there." She pointed her trowel here and there.

Julian stared, bug-eyed. "To quote Lewis Carroll, 'Begin at the beginning and go on till you come to the end, then stop.' About last night…?"

She sucked in a deep breath. "I was waiting for the train in Covent Garden Station—it was late. I'd gone to the pub with a few friends after class. The platform was quiet, just me and a couple of others, waiting for the train. I became aware of a vibration, a kind of throbbing pressure in my eardrums. A few seconds later I saw it—huge and powerful with large fangs and flashing eyes. The creature slowed a bit and stared straight at me."

"Holy shit, you made eye contact." One of the things she dearly loved about Julian was his devotion to all things otherworldly. He wasn't just a fan boy of *Buffy the Vampire Slayer*, he wanted to be Buffy. Elle wondered if technically that made him a fan girl.

"Honestly, my knees were shaking. The beast streaked through the platform, leapt onto the tracks, and disappeared into the tunnel. Moments later I heard terrible shrieks and cries. As if someone was being tortured or worse."

Julian swallowed. "Mauled, perhaps?"

She nodded. "I dug for my phone, dialed 999 and ran."

"But you made a police report." Julian eyed her skeptically.

"I stopped at Ebury Station on my way home. I must be the only one who reported seeing the creature. The officer wanted details, but the image was already fading."

"What did you describe?"

"Just…a very large black dog." Elle returned to vigorous digging.

Julian squinted. "And what do you think it really was?"

She leaned across the bed. "A werewolf—I'm sure of it."

His nod was cute and conspiratorial. "Definitely a were."

Chapter

TWO

The Lord of Westminster summons his brother,
D.I. Abelseth Durant.

Stirred up, Abelseth waited impatiently for the train to Westminster.

Essence of wolfen had pervaded Chelsea Physic Garden. He refocused his senses, concentrating on the mystery of her scent—top notes of ylang ylang over a base of airy musk.

Ms. Elle Hathaway had awakened the beast inside.

Lycanthrope pheromones brought back pleasure as well as pain. The loyalty and warmth of his pack, the intimate bonding and ferocious mating. Then came the painful recollection of his brother's betrayal and the needless mayhem that followed after.

He shook off the memory, careful not to shift in the process.

Inexplicably, he turned toward the pedestrian tunnel that led up to street level. A figure emerged, partially hidden in the bend of the passageway.

His nostrils flared and pupils dilated. For the second time today, he sensed…wolf.

Long time, Abelseth.

He drew closer and recognized his cousin. "Phelan?"

Forever posh, even in rumpled evening attire. His cousin was exceedingly good looking, almost ridiculously so. "Hard night of clubbing? Recently booted out of a West End girl's flat?"

"Must it be one or the other?" His cousin's twisted grin appeared wistful, yet cunning. "Can't it be both?"

"Once a rogue always a rogue."

Phelan exhaled an impatient sigh. "Shall we skip the niceties?"

There was so much to like about his cousin—his brains, his bravado, his acerbic wit. And yet, from the time they were both cubs, he'd always sensed a deep melancholy in Phelan.

"Grim times. Maccon has called a conclave and he wants you there."

"It's been five years." He shook his head. "I'm out."

"Abelseth, son of Aethelwulf—from the noble blood rulers of Wessex—once and forever lords of the clan." Phelan stepped in close. "You're never out."

A rush of corpuscles mutated. Nanoseconds of excruciating pain. Abelseth grew fangs and his snout elongated. *Good Christ—a partial shift.* With his teeth gnashing, he snapped at his irritating cousin.

Phelan yelped and circled him.

Eyes riveted on his cousin, fangs dripping saliva, Abelseth managed to pull himself together with a body shake. He was no longer duty-bound to his pack, but he would always be fated to them. The binding nature of wolf culture would forever call to him—it was inescapable.

"Tonight," Phelan snarled, wiping spittle from his topcoat. "You've been summoned." His cousin shifted in and out of the drift, appearing inside a railcar as the train left the station.

Cursing under his breath, Abelseth walked back to the platform and waited for the next train. He was sloppy, out of practice. His partial shift showed a rare loss of control and could have exposed him in public.

Maccon would use that to his advantage if he thought he could provoke him. Well, he refused to be lured into one of his brother's nefarious plots. "You've been summoned," he muttered sarcastically. Unstable lycanthrope particles continued to vibrate inside his body.

Every shift was visceral and tantalizing, a taste of the life he'd left behind. During his years away from London proper, he'd kept a strict regimen. Once a week he'd go for a long four-legged run. Enough to rid his body of the primitive urges that plagued his kind.

Before accepting the position with Metropolitan Police CID, he'd made a promise to himself. Never again would he get lured into the mayhem and madness of the city's wolfen underworld.

He was a lone wolf. And he was going to stay that way.

The train ride was brief. Three stops to the Westminster tube station, then a block and a half walk to headquarters. New Scotland Yard had recently been restored to its rightful place on the Victoria Embankment. Not unlike himself, the Metropolitan

Police had come full circle and returned home. He took the lift to the fourth floor and entered a large, bustling office space.

"Good day, Ms. Kendall. Busy morning?"

"Madhouse—two high profile suicides, and five suspicious deaths. Call me Cara." He caught the wink in the attractive clerk's smile.

"It's called job security, Ms. Kendall." Abelseth hung his coat on a hook by his desk.

"You've got several messages, check your inbox," she called after him. "And it's Cara." Her gaze roamed over his backside. The young woman was incorrigible.

He settled into his cubicle and opened his email. Nothing that required an immediate response. Crime Scene had yet to post their report on the mauling. Perhaps he'd pay Dermot Crowley a visit in person.

He opened the case file and uploaded Ms. Hathaway's police report.

Everything about the incident in the tube made Abelseth uneasy. On the job for less than a month and already he suspected one of the wolf packs was behind the mauling. An attack on a civilian was bold and unnerving. Perhaps Phelan was right. Grim times.

"Our resident Essex girl says you've got sex symbol hair." Gordon Murray stood in the cubicle entrance looking overly suave.

"That's absurd, don't be—come on—sex symbol hair?" Abelseth snorted a laugh. "Because it's a bit long and I can toss it about?"

Gordon appeared miffed, or jealous. His poncy

coworker had the inflated idea he was the Yard's most dashing detective, and it amused Abelseth to encourage him. Something about the private ruse made Gordon's insufferable opinion of himself bearable.

He returned to his report, half-listening to the detective rattle on. Perhaps now was the time to see if Dermot Crowley had any preliminary thoughts.

Abelseth rose from his desk and sidestepped Gordon. "Don't you have a case to work on?"

"The suspect confessed. She claims she got sucked into the Matrix, so she stabbed her landlady in the heart." Gordon walked over to Crime Scene with him. "Mind if I tag along?"

The bright shock of ginger hair was unmistakable. Dermot Crowley was in. Abelseth peered over the top of his partition. "Mr. Crowley, have a moment?"

The CS investigator looked up from his monitor. "You're the new man over in—?"

"Homicide Task Force, Abelseth Durant. I'm on the mauling case."

"What, you blokes after a pack of pit bulls?" Gordon scoffed.

"My report is nearly complete," Crowley huffed. "I'll send over top line remarks in a few minutes." The CS man turned to Gordon. "Rather a perturbing case, actually. No evidence of a pack of dogs, yet the torn flesh and number of bites would suggest otherwise."

"We may have a witness." Abelseth brightened. "A report came in early this morning—mentioned a large black dog running loose in the Covent Garden tube. I'm going to question the young woman this afternoon, anything I should ask?"

Crowley scrolled through his notes. "The case seems fairly straightforward on the surface and yet—"

"Was the victim on the run from a dog or some other pursuer?" Abelseth shared some of the questions racing around in his head. "Or was this purely an accident—marauding canines on the hunt? And if not, what was the victim doing in the train tunnel?"

"No wallet, no identification. There is a bit of evidence you might follow up on." Crowley opened a file of photos on his computer. "See here—the victim's clothing was torn to shreds, but his suit label suggests a man of means."

Abelseth squinted. "Gieves & Hawkes."

Gordon blew a soft whistle. "Savile Row. A man found mauled to death in the tube wearing a custom-tailored suit. Things are getting interesting."

"Anything from Traffic, yet?" Abelseth asked.

"We've requested CCTV on the platform and station entrance. Footage should be here later today."

Abelseth returned to his desk and made a few phone calls, one to the Savile Row tailor and another to the coroner's office. Crowley sent over his preliminary report and he spent the rest of the day sifting through the findings. Shortly after three o'clock, he packed it in and set off for his teatime appointment.

A curious excitement elevated his pulse. Elle Hathaway was not obviously pretty, and yet she took his breath away. Whenever she smiled or spoke, her features came alive. And there was a directness about her—a quiet boldness that had caught him off guard.

Long, unkempt waves had continually escaped from a messy bun. He'd swept burnished wheat-colored locks off her cheek and made a startling connection. Her eyes were a lovely shade of green—rich and unsettling, with flecks of gold that shimmered, even on a gray morning. He'd averted his gaze, only to be captivated by a wide, sensuous mouth. Lips that promised unholy pleasures and a torrid exchange of body fluids.

He gave himself a good shake, head to tail.

"Wolfsbane," she'd warned, wiggling gloved fingers. It wouldn't be his first encounter with a beautiful wolf hunter.

Chapter

THREE

Tea for two and two for tea.

Elle kicked off her wellies and carefully removed goggles, gloves, and overalls. Protective clothing got tossed into the laundry chute, everything else would be hosed down and left on a drying rack.

"You run along, I've got this." Julian pressed the trigger on the nozzle and sprayed down her gear. "Elle, you'll be late for your date with Detective Inspector Dreamy."

"It's not a date. It's an interrogation."

Julian flashed a smirking, one-sided smile. "Don't let him cuff you, unless you want him to."

She dashed for the lockers and took a quick shower—scrubbing, rinsing, and repinning her hair. She opened her locker and checked her watch. "Shit. Crap." In a flash, she pulled on a sweater, tugged on leggings, and stepped into booties on her way out the door.

Elle took a shortcut through the culinary garden and entered Tangerine Dream by way of the dining patio. Outside the front entrance, she spied a tall figure wearing a long coat. She paused for moment, just to look at him.

She'd forgotten how attractive he was, in an unkempt masculine way. With his collar up and his faraway gaze, he reminded her of the statue of Sir Hans Sloane, the celebrated physician proudly brooding in the center of the garden.

Lucy sidled up next to her. "Who's the dishy devil with the sex symbol hair?"

"Detective Inspector Durant."

"He's waiting for you?"

Elle turned and stared. "Would you mind not looking so surprised?"

"It's about time you dropped your knickers." Lucy waltzed away. "And for a sexy copper—nice one, Elle."

She opened her mouth to correct her cheeky coworker, then bit her tongue. The thought of something wet and wild with the detective gave her the tingles. She sucked in a breath and opened the front door of the cafe.

He pivoted. "Ms. Hathaway."

"Much cozier inside, Inspector."

She led the way past a bakery display filled with tarts and cakes to a window table overlooking a small pond. "Private enough?"

The detective did a cursory inspection of the near empty tearoom. "This will be fine."

They'd barely settled in when Lucy showed up, wearing a flirty smile. "Hello, Elle." She turned to the inspector and gave him a thorough once-over. "What can I get for the two of you?"

He pulled off his scarf. "Do you prefer tea or coffee?"

For a man with such lovely blue eyes, his gaze was difficult to return. A girl could drown in those liquid crystalline orbs. Perhaps they were the reason she always felt slightly out of breath around him.

"Definitely tea in the afternoon." She managed a weak smile.

"Shall I order a pot of Earl Grey?"

"Perfect!" Lucy blurted out before she could answer. "Back in a flash."

He shrugged out of his coat. She thought he dressed rather well, if somewhat conservatively. Charcoal gray shirt with a darker gray tie, loosened enough to move her evaluation of his dress to conservative, with touches of casual confidence.

"Hard day, or just a long day, Inspector?"

His unsettling gaze never wavered. "More of a puzzling day."

She brightened. "An average day then, for a Yard man."

The ends of his mouth curled upward. "I wouldn't call it average, either."

Lucy brought a steaming pot of tea to the table, along with a clatter of cups and saucers. "Sorry, don't know what's got into me today. I'm all thumbs and dropsies. Can I get you anything else? A lavender scone with clotted cream? The lemon tarts are lovely."

It seemed Lucy could barely take her eyes off the handsome detective; so much so, she'd gone all thumbs and dropsies.

Elle flattened a grin. "I'd love a slice of brownie cake."

"Brownie cake?" The detective arched a brow.

"A dense chocolate cake with chocolate drops and nuts," she explained.

Lucy put in a nod. "Scrummy."

"Make that two."

"Two it is—would you like me to warm them up?" Lucy asked.

He shifted his gaze to their frisky waitress. "By all means."

She stared at him slightly open-mouthed. He was flirting—with her and Lucy. Detective Inspector Durant was a hottie and he knew it. What remained in his favor, she supposed, was that he didn't seem to pay much attention to his looks, hence the unkemptness, nor did he appear overly impressed with himself.

He sat quietly in front of her, consulting his smartphone.

"New Scotland Yard has gone paperless—rather high tech of them, wouldn't you say?"

He cleared his throat softly. "I thought we might start with your police report. You can confirm, make corrections, elaborate—whatever comes to mind." He glanced up at her. "If you need clarification, feel free to ask me anything."

Elle immediately thought of two good questions: Have a girlfriend? Looking for one? Instead, she lifted a small pitcher. "Milk?"

"Just a spot." He stirred slowly as he read aloud. "Name: Ms. Luella Hathaway. Gender: Female. Address: 3 Groom Place, Belgravia." He arched a brow at the upscale address.

"I've an arrangement with the owner of 17 Chester Street, a Mr. Mokhtaar."

"Foreign?"

"Algerian, originally. He lives in Dubai now, spends less than four months a year in London. Last winter the house was completely restored, kitchen and loos updated. He also had a brilliant roof garden designed with a glass house full of rare orchids." She sipped her tea. "I get the apartment above the garage—"

He surmised the rest. "In exchange for the care and feeding of his exotic flora." Beneath the surface of those arresting blue eyes, wheels turned. And his double take was lovely, as if he must have another look at her.

Tingles again—tits to nethers.

He made a few notes and continued on. "Late in the evening, on March twenty-one, Ms. Hathaway witnessed a dog racing along the track as she stood, alone, waiting for a train on the Piccadilly Line. She described the canine as very large with black fur—longish coat—glowing eyes and pointed teeth. She believes the creature slowed and looked in her direction before vanishing into the south tunnel." He reached the end of her statement and looked up. "Quite an unusual encounter, yet you waited until after you returned to Belgravia to report the incident."

"Frankly, I debated whether or not to report it at all."

"Then why did you, Ms. Hathaway?"

The deep blackness of the tunnel returned to her as if she were standing on the platform. Flashing yellow eyes, gnashing teeth, and then the cry. She raised her gaze. "I believe it was the awful chilling scream. Bloody bloodcurdling, actually."

"Bloody bloodcurdling." His teasing smile faded as he scrolled through several pages on his phone. "You made no mention of a scream."

She craned her neck to see his notes. "I distinctly remember a scream—several of them—strange I didn't think to report it." She chewed her lower lip.

His gaze dropped to her mouth. "Very often a witness to a crime will remember events with greater clarity after the shock has passed."

"Crime?" She swallowed. "The person who was attacked is…?"

He stared at me. "Dead, I'm afraid."

Elle gasped. "I never saw—how awful—"

The detective nodded. "Mauled quite badly. Poor bloke never stood a chance."

Lucy arrived at the table and set down two plates, along with forks, and a custard cup of clotted cream. "Enjoy your brownie cakes, baked fresh this morning." As she backed away, she gave Elle a girlfriend-to-girlfriend wink.

The detective resumed questioning between bites. "The body was found in the south tunnel no more than one hundred feet from the station. The cries you heard must have been the attack. Can you recall anything else out of the ordinary?"

When she blanked, he pushed for more description. "Might there have been more than one canine—a pack for instance?"

"I didn't see another dog. I suppose there could

have been more than one."

"Were there any other sounds, besides the screams?"

Elle closed her eyes and went deeper into the tunnel. "Perhaps there was a bark or two—and growls. Nothing like the screams, though."

"And you would characterize this event—the cries and growls as lasting for how long…approximately?"

She sensed something rare in the detective. A spark of something primitive and feral smoldered in reserve. "Interminable, terrifying cries. I dialed 999, and ran from the station. I took the night bus home."

"May I ask what you were doing in Covent Garden?"

"I was returning home from a dance lesson."

"Name and address of the academy, if you would?"

"Pineapple Studios on Langley Street."

He sat back and studied her. "What…sort of dance?"

She narrowed her gaze. The inspector had suddenly gone far off topic, nevertheless, he did appear genuinely interested. "Lyrical Dance. It's a combination of—"

"Sorry to be a bother," Lucy interrupted, "but the cafe is closing." She placed the bill on the table. "Would you mind, so I can close the till?"

The detective paid the check, and left a substantial tip. "I'd like to get a bit more description on the attack dog, if I may. You described a large, shaggy canine. More collie or German Shepherd?"

"German Shepherd."

"More German Shepherd or wolf?"

She swallowed. "Wolf."

His pupils dilated. A strange energy broke loose inside Elle. It was as though he held her captive in his gaze. She felt dizzy, and the tingles were back. No man had ever made her feel this way. At twenty-five, Elle was beginning to think no man ever would.

A knowing is how her mother described it. "I just knew when I met your father, Elle."

Could this be one of those knowing moments? The attraction she felt was so strong she nearly forgot to breathe. No matter, there was little oxygen left in the room.

His phone rang and broke the spell.

"D.I. Durant." He continued to make eye contact. "At this hour, twenty minutes. I'm in Chelsea." He pocketed his phone. "Duty calls, I'm afraid."

A wave of loss washed over her. This whole attraction thing with the inspector, and now this bereft feeling. What exactly was she experiencing?

As they rose to leave, Lucy called out her. "Girls night out, tonight—or did you forget? South London Soul Train at XOYO."

Elle smiled. "Pick you up at nine." Being socially challenged herself, she'd come to admire Lucy's hook-up skills. If the detective was interested, he knew exactly where to find them this evening.

Outside the cafe, he handed her his card. "If anything pops up, the smallest detail, ring me at this number."

"Abelseth Durant." She grinned. "Poor man, even worse than Luella. My friends call me Elle. What on earth do your friends call you?"

147

The way he arched that eyebrow was positively breathtaking. "My friends call me Abelseth."

Elle gave herself a mental slap. "No doubt a family name with a long and noble history."

He continued to study her. Between Lucy's flirtation and her own awkward rudeness, the mixed messages must be dizzying. An icy wind gusted under the Inspector's scarf, and it billowed up in the air.

"Here, let me." Elle caught one end of the scarf. "I'm good with these." She folded the length in half and pulled the ends through the loop, tightening the scarf around his neck.

He observed her every move, each turn and twist of his neckwear. "There, not too neat, you want to look casual." She ended up standing quite close to him. Her gaze trailed up the scarf and connected with his lovely eyes.

"Watch yourself tonight." He spoke softly, almost intimately. "There were two abductions in Shoreditch last week, both officially charged as missing persons."

A parting shot of tingly. "I promise to be careful, Inspector Durant."

He lingered a moment before he turned to leave. "Good evening, Ms. Hathaway."

Chapter

FOUR

West End girls and East End wolves.

Abelseth descended into the belly of the beast. He prepared for sensory overload and adjusted inner ear auditory nerves.

Soul music mingled with disco and nineties pop; the deejay's own special mix of electronica. And the sound system at XOYO went well beyond a good ear swoon. From under a sprung dance floor, the thumping baseline vibrated through bodies in motion.

Damn his wolfen soul to hell.

Hot, damp pheromones assaulted his olfactory sensors, while disco balls turned and laser lights flashed over young singles on the prowl. His nose twitched as he wove a path through the crowded rom.

There—the flirtatious waitress from the cafe rubbed up against some bloke covered in ink. Pretty, but not really his type. He preferred…no sign of her as yet.

Abelseth headed for the bar and ordered a shot of single malt. He needed something to dull his animal senses, and whiskey didn't mess about. He found a spot at the bar that wasn't three deep and enjoyed the liquid amber burn. Airy strings dissolved into the thump, thump, thump, of a disco beat. He searched bobbing heads illuminated by slashes of laser light.

There—he found her—hair flying, hips rocking, mouth slightly open. A living, breathing wet dream.

This afternoon in the cafe, Elle had become a distraction with every sip of tea, every bite of cake. She'd licked crumbs from the edge of her lips, and he'd discovered the permanent upturn at the corners of her mouth. Disarming and sensuous, the allure of Elle Hathaway had quickly become irresistible. After watching the CCTV footage, he'd gone home, taken a shower, and fantasized about doing bad things with her in the dark, with or without a bed.

Closed circuit images had clearly shown Elle standing in the Underground waiting for the train. Another group of four waited further down the platform. At 10:55, Elle's body language noticeably changed before being obscured by static interference. When the video noise cleared, the camera caught a glimpse of her, cell phone in hand, as she exited the station. He'd gone over and over the recordings.

Someone gave him a nudge. "Hello, luv."

The scent of vanilla mingled with tobacco. Elle's friend Lucy rubbed against his shoulder. He dipped his head closer to hear.

"Aren't you mad swagger in leather and black denim."

"Mad swagger?" He snorted in protest.

"And you pulled your hair back, samurai style." She gave him a serious once-over. "A hundred percent mad swagger."

The disc jockey mixed something breathy

and seductive into the edgy beat of a Spice Girls throwback tune. The electronic siren whispered her sultry command: *Closer, baby.*

He half-listened to Lucy while keeping an eye on Elle. He had two choices this evening. Attend his brother's summons, or trot after the clubbing females—one in particular.

Lucy gave his sleeve a tug. "Slip out for a fag with me?"

A bit too quickly, he encouraged her absence. "You go ahead, but don't flirt with strange men."

"I came here to flirt with strange men." Lucy pouted.

"Yes, of course." His gaze narrowed. "Just… watch yourself."

"Cheeky copper." The girl pushed off the bar and disappeared into the crowd.

A lush tropical cloud of ylang ylang transfixed his nostrils. Drawn to the intoxicating scent of Elle, he set his glass down and zigzagged through undulating bodies.

She moved with the utter joy and abandon of someone born to dance. Coppery wheat-colored waves flew around her head, and when she dipped low and rolled her hips, he experienced a strong urge to rub up against her.

The breathy electronic voice moaned under thumping beats. *Closer, baby.*

Elle swung around, bringing them face to face. There was a brief delay before she gasped. "Inspector Durant." Cheeks flushed from exertion, she tossed waves of hair off her face, soft and wild. After dancing effortlessly, she suddenly appeared to be out of breath.

"You look…" Her gaze swept over him. "…lovely."

Her skin glowed under a sheen of perspiration. Stunned momentarily, he failed to return her compliment. She smiled. "Dance with me?"

"I don't dance."

The entire bar erupted in cheers as a crescendo of guitar notes blasted out of the sound system. The throbbing, infectious beat of retro disco. Inebriated dancers crowded onto the dance floor, pushing them together.

"You don't dance?" Elle drew a plump bottom lip under her teeth.

Bass notes bumped underfoot as light waves slashed overhead. He should back away, disappear into the throng of dancers. In the morning, slightly hungover, she'd wonder if she'd seen him at all.

Instead, he yanked her into his arms and felt the warmth of her gasp.

Nostrils flared, pupils dilated, as his gaze lowered to her lips. "Don't bite your lip, let me do that for you." He nipped at her pouty mouth.

Good Christ, the taste of her.

If he wasn't careful, his wolf lust would shred those luscious lips. He licked the sensitive curve of her cupid's bow. "I didn't mean to—"

"I know what you meant." Elle caught the edge of his lip between her teeth, and scraped. Surprised by her fearless, seductive taunt, he stepped back.

She rolled her body against him, and he placed his

hands on her hips. She dipped lower, and he rocked with her pelvis to pelvis.

"I thought you didn't dance."

"We aren't dancing, we're grinding." His gaze revisited her mouth.

Raw, swollen lips surrendered as he brushed his mouth over hers in a slow, possessive assault. Gentler this time, with sensuous tongue play. When he finally broke off the kiss, they were both panting.

She stepped away, raising her arms in sultry surrender. Rocking her hips side to side, she swung around and deliberately brushed that cute booty against him.

He held onto her hips and moved with her, nuzzling her ear. "I feel a sin coming on."

Elle's skirt fluttered up, tempting his fingers under the hem. Her breathy moan dared him to go further— to the edge of her thong. His hand swept up the back of her thigh and cupped a sweet curve of bouncing flesh…

Good Bloody Christ. Abelseth broke away.

She'd ignited a seething, feral arousal he wasn't prepared for. He reminded himself to breathe and gulped in air. What was he thinking? The simple answer—he wasn't. And he had no trouble reading Elle's delayed reaction.

The inspector had his hand on my bum—the wanker.

Wobbling a bit, she reached out and he steadied her. A hunger this powerful could cause a shift. And he'd broken away too quickly, leaving them both disoriented.

Elle shivered in his arms. Odd, that she would be so deeply affected. He nuzzled silken waves, and inhaled her scent. From the moment he'd swept stray hairs off her cheek in the garden, he'd detected a whiff of his kind.

He held on tighter, rocking her gently back and forth. Darling girl. As her trembling eased, she mouthed words he couldn't hear. Finally, she pointed in the general direction of the loo.

He took hold of her hand and ran interference. Men and women alike moved in and out of the facilities. With the afterburn of Elle simmering in his blood, he suddenly hated unisex toilets. Dodgy shag bogs of iniquity. If he accompanied her inside, he might do something unthinkable.

He pulled her close. "I owe you an apology. That booty grab was uncalled for."

Pretty, slightly bruised lips curled into a bashful grin. "Not…completely uncalled for." Her hand slipped from his. "Wait for me?"

He followed her with his eyes. *Right where you left me.*

Abelseth braced himself against brick and mortar. He'd lost control over a kiss. He sucked in a breath and exhaled slowly. Little by little, his scrambled sensory abilities realigned.

How could he have been so wrong about her? Elle was beyond gorgeous, and as delicious as she was daring. Never in his life had he experienced anything quite like what had just happened on the dance floor. He might have torn her clothes off in the middle of bloody *Disco Inferno*.

At first he'd suspected wolf hunter. Clever stalkers often doused themselves in lycanthrope pheromones. But now that he'd tasted her, Elle was pure, uninitiated wolfen. He was sure of it.

There were stories of wolf-blooded humans able to resist the change for years. And new drugs were available, lycanthrope suppressants that tamed the inner beast. Might they also be able to delay the onset of change?

Fear has an acrid, metallic odor, and something was making his nose twitch. He zeroed in on the roof patio, up several flights of stairs.

Elle's friend.

He took two steps at a time, squeezing through a crowd of smokers. He ignored the toxic fumes and found Lucy near the roof ledge, sitting on the tattooed bloke's lap. The same tosser he'd seen her dancing with earlier.

Confused, he backed away. His senses hadn't stabilized. Unless…clearly sensing wolf, he pivoted back toward those muscled arms covered in ink.

Abelseth stepped back in play. "Lucy, here you are. Elle's been looking for you. We're off to Cargo—come with." He didn't wait for an answer, he grabbed her hand and pulled her off the bruiser.

"Hold on, the bird's with me, bloody bastard." The able bodied man sprang to his feet.

"Listen, mate, avoid getting emotional." Abelseth pushed Lucy behind him and held up both hands. "It always backfires when blokes try to fight me. You'll always, always lose. It's also bad for seduction, the bouncers will never let you take the girl home—"

Lucy gave his jacket a hard yank from behind and they raced down the stairs. "Nice of you to come along, Inspector." She tossed the words over her shoulder. "He's a hot hook-up, but a bit scary."

Abelseth frowned. "Piece of advice, don't sit on any bloke's lap you'd describe as 'a bit scary.'"

They reached the bottom of the stairs, and he directed her into the loo. "Find Elle for me."

The stink of rival wolfen was about. East Enders, likely Gryffins or worse, Ex Cereberus.

Senses on alert, he waited outside the lavatory for both young women. In the crowded club, scents mingled and merged, nearly impossible to track a lone wolf on the prowl.

A flicker at the edge of his vision gave him pause. And he failed to breathe a sigh of relief when both Elle and Lucy walked up to him, lipstick freshly applied.

Elle studied him, brows knitted. "What's wrong?"

"Nothing," he reassured her blithely. "Just...glad to see you."

She brightened. "I hear you're taking us to Cargo."

"Better crowd. And they serve aged single malt, humor me?"

Any man leaving the club with these two lovely creatures was bound to attract attention. Between the coat check and sidewalk, he received a number of glances. Even the bouncer seemed impressed.

Lucy and Elle had a laugh over it. "Bloody pervs."

Elle fished a valet ticket out of her pocket.

"You've a car?" He arched a brow.

Air whipped up around them, the kind of whoosh

one felt from a tube vent underfoot. The scent of wolf was thick in the evening mist.

An orange Mini Cooper with matte black racing stripes pulled up to the curb. Abelseth stared. "You splendid girl."

"I don't often drive when we go clubbing. I hope we have a designated driver?"

"That would be me." He gestured toward the sporty compact.

Lucy climbed into the backseat, and he stepped aside to let Elle in the front. Another strong disturbance of air buffeted around him. The physical universe was being altered in a sneaky way, so as not to alarm civilians.

"Elle?" He spun around and caught a glimpse of shimmer–the flutter of her skirt. Feet shuffled and there was a muffled cry, but mostly he heard the frenetic beat of her heart. And all of it came from just around the corner.

He dove inside the sporty car, gunned the engine and whipped a U-turn. "They've got Elle."

Tossed from one side of the car to the other, Lucy grabbed hold of the front seat headrest. "Who's got Elle?" She gasped, panic in her voice.

Facing on-coming traffic, Abelseth jumped the curb and drove down the sidewalk. Nothing but dark storefronts. He slowed the car to peer inside a dimly lit vape shop. Whoever had taken her would go to ground, and he couldn't risk missing their escape route.

"Inspector, what's going on?" Lucy insisted.

"No time for chat, we need to find them quickly.

157

Look for open manholes, empty shops to-let, basement gates, doors left ajar…"

"I believe there's a ghost stop back up the road. They're converting the station into a skate park."

Abelseth slammed on the brakes and threw the car in reverse.

"There—" Lucy pointed down the narrow cross street. "The old Shoreditch Station." He parked under a street lamp and killed the engine. He could just make out the name carved in stone above the boarded-up entrance.

"Stay in the car. Do not open a door or window for anyone."

C h a p t e r

FIVE

Elle comes face to face with a pack of wolves.

Icy talons of wind swept Elle off the street and into the shadows. Her cries had been swallowed up in a cyclone of whirling lampposts. Neon signs and shop fronts too blurry or dark to make sense of.

She was either moving very fast, or very slow. And she felt nothing, just a strange pressure at the back of her head and neck. Super strong and male, her captor held her in his grip. And there was another, an accomplice who prodded her forward. Stumbling over pavers, she tried to wrench away, but her legs wobbled as a peculiar lethargy washed over her.

In the midst of an out of body stupor, she watched her suede booties get dragged across wet cobblestones. They entered a dark alley full of dank smells. Her nose twitched from the scent of toasted marshmallows—a vape odor.

Dragged down a flight stairs, she managed to wriggle out of the oafish man's grip. "Fierce one aren't you? Probably have a tight little cunt, as well." He tossed her over his shoulder like she was a sack of potting soil.

Elle's temples throbbed as blood rushed to her

head. Her limp, rag doll body swayed with every turn in the passageway. Glimpses of upside down advertisements, tiled walls, the crunch of gravel underfoot.

More darkness.

They were in the Underground, she was almost sure of it. Another round of off-putting odors. The brittle clink of footsteps on metal—perhaps a catwalk or stairs.

And what of her friends? She imagined Inspector Durant and Lucy standing on the curb, completely gobsmacked, wondering where she'd disappeared to.

Harsh knocks and the whine of hinges jolted her into sharper awareness. A heavy door opened and closed. Thick, intricately patterned carpet muffled the big oaf's footsteps.

Elle fought to stay alert, to make sense of her captor's mumbled conversation. She had arrived somewhere, but where?

*

Abelseth sniffed the air. Hints of luscious Elle with top notes of adrenaline. Underneath her human scent, the tantalizing musk of wolfen. He sensed a struggle as well.

The bonny girl was putting up a fight.

As he approached the station entrance, a gust of frigid air rattled the doors. Elle's abduction had been a public grab, as risky as it was audacious. Had to be either Gryffins or Ex Cereberus—Exers for short. And since both packs were known for their stealth, the obvious scent trail meant they were expecting him.

He slipped his fingers between the entry doors, shifted nails to wolf claws, and ripped through the lock and chain. He entered the deserted station and descended the stairs to the platform.

Under the aquiline noses of kings and queens, London packs had thrived above and below ground for centuries. The Wolf Lords of Westminster, the oldest and most prestigious of all the packs, currently occupied seats in both Houses of Parliament—two of them rising stars in the Tory cabinet.

Above ground, his brother Maccon Durant, an investment banker and venture capitalist, managed all of the Lords' holdings, as well as building wealth for the greater Pendragon clan.

Abelseth sidestepped a slippery pool of sludge.

Below city streets, the packs shared a private labyrinth of Roman catacombs, underground rivers and secret passages built for trysts between kings and mistresses. And if you knew where to look—ancient wolfen halls.

He dropped onto the tracks and easily picked up their trail. This whole thing was his fault. He'd blown off his brother's summons, possibly goading Maccon into a threatening assault on Elle.

Don't fuck with me, brother.

Message received.

Abduction was not something wolves took lightly. Abelseth bit back his anger. Then again, she was a beautiful, innocent female. And it wouldn't be the first time Maccon had stolen a potential mate from him.

He came to a lurching halt mid-stride. Cannabis fumes assaulted his olfactory senses. Hovering in and around the strong scent, a barely perceptible whiff of his kind.

A wisp of mist hung over the train tracks. The sound of rippling water meant that an underground river was close. He also sensed a larger body of water, perhaps one of the old canals, nearby. He used the sound of running water to calm his pounding heart, and soon the clink and rattle of footsteps on metal, came through clearly.

He turned slowly and squinted.

There—a passageway, barely a niche in the wall. A quick search revealed a utility door spray painted with cryptic characters. WLW 04. Roughly Translated: Wolf Lords of Westminster. There were nine secret meeting places under the City of London. Abelseth could not recall ever attending a gathering in 04.

He reached in his pocket for his passkey and unlocked the door. The sweet pungent scent of ganja nearly knocked him over as he stepped into the underground farm.

Grow lights illuminated a hundred meters of leafy green tunnel in each direction. Asian street gangs leased lengthy sections of abandoned tube from the wolfen. As a result, London's potheads had their pick of Agent Orange, Death Star, Russian White or Trainwreck, all of them potent strains of smoke. Rumor had it the gangs changed up flavors in the same way Starbucks created seasonal lattes.

His nose twitched and it wasn't from the pot farm.

Elle was close.

He continued to puzzle over her abduction. On the face of it, an absurd, ridiculous overreaction to his snubbing. There had to be another, more pressing motive, as to why Elle ended up on their radar. The fact that any pack had an inkling about her was curious, indeed.

Abelseth picked his way through rows of mature plants, ready for harvest.

"Hold on—who the fuck are you?"

His pivot brought his nose dangerously close to the tip of a samurai sword. At the opposite end of the blade, a very large Asian gentleman stared him down.

"Abelseth Durant." He held up his hands in surrender. "Maccon Durant is my brother. I've been called to a rather urgent meeting. Somehow I got turned around—lovely farm by the way—I'm looking for the wolf hall. You wouldn't happen to know where it is…by any chance?"

The gang member was likely part of the cannabis farm's night watch. Eyeing him suspiciously, the sumo-sized man relented with a grunt. "Wait here."

Abelseth gave him a few seconds, then followed on behind in stealth mode.

*

One by one, Elle memorized each detail of the hall she was being held in. Low, vaulted ceilings supported by plain Doric columns. Ancient Persian carpets. Several large tapestries hung on the walls—

two of them told tales of heroic battles, while a third depicted a festival, complete with jousts and jugglers. The tapestries had one thing in common, all the knights were dressed in battle armor with exquisitely detailed, oddly shaped helmets. Long snouts, eye holes shaded by a slash of metal that arched and came to points over the ears. The effect was eerily stunning. Woven into the richly textured border were the words: *Ordo lupus Domini. Loyal au mort.*

The Order of Wolf Lords. Loyal unto death.

Being a botanist had its advantages, like being able to translate dead languages.

Other than some rough manhandling, the band of thugs hadn't touched Elle in a sexual way. Several men had circled her, then quickly retreated, as if they'd been warned off or threatened. Frankly, it made her wonder.

"Would one of you mind telling me why I'm here? If it's ransom you're after, I can assure you I've no money and neither does my family."

No answer from her captors, just sullen looks.

One of her abductors had questioned her briefly about Inspector Durant. He'd also mentioned a man known to her and other like-minded wolfen as The Chemist. Her abductors even knew the name of her London distributor. Iggy Binns.

Elle shivered. She'd tricked herself into believing she could disrupt her DNA and lead a normal life. But little more than a day or two off the lycanthrope suppressant, they'd found her out.

A long table and chairs occupied the center of the meeting space. At one end, a hearth threw a bit of heat onto the men standing close by.

A medieval boardroom filled with courtiers and their captive. Best case scenario, they were waiting for their lord on high to arrive. Worst case? An interrogator or torturer.

Torturer. Horrible thought.

Her gaze traveled over the tall, muscled males. Despite their obvious boorishness, they were all attractive men. With the kind of physique that aroused interest from women who should know better.

The word enforcers came to mind. Special operations, black ops kind of men who did their duty without question. They all took turns staring at her, but said very little, even amongst themselves.

Elle had nothing to bargain with until she knew what they wanted. She had an inkling that her capture might have as much to do with Inspector Durant as herself, though she placed little trust in the flash of insight. The shock of her abduction may have worn off, but her brain was still a bit fuzzy. Even so, she wondered. Was Abelseth Durant friend or foe…or something else entirely?

The men at the far end of the room appeared to be curious, but she also read suspicion in their sullen looks and darting glances. One of them sauntered over and eyed her as if she were an artifact in a rare collection.

Without a word, he wrinkled up his nose. "There is something about her…" He leaned closer and sniffed the air.

"Bite her and be done with it." One of the men taunted him.

"Nasty business, abducting females. And I'm afraid you'd be wasting your time. The young lady would very likely bite back."

Inspector Durant stood in the center of the room. He appeared relaxed and confident, even when surrounded.

Her heart pounded and those prickly tingles were back. He'd come for her, and it was as thrilling as it was terrifying.

The inspector turned toward an Asian man standing by the entry door and bowed. "Thank you, sumo warrior with the long sword." The door slammed shut by itself and Inspector Durant became a blur.

He reappeared beside her, holding the man's samurai sword with two hands as he faced down her abductors.

Elle sensed fear from the men and a strange sort of deferential awe. An extremely handsome man, wearing an expensive suit, approached the inspector. "You're looking posh, with your Jared Leto hair. Have you suddenly become *au courant*, Abelseth?" Behind him, the others closed in, including the large bull who'd tossed her over his shoulder.

Seemingly unfazed by the men surrounding him, Inspector Durant lowered his sword. "*Au courant—* you mean in the fashion sense?"

Elle had seen some masterful brow arches from the inspector, but this one amused her.

"And why such interest in my hair? I can't fathom it. This morning it was sex symbol hair, and now Jared Leto hair. Complete nonsense since there is a more pressing problem at hand, namely Ms. Hathaway."

He appeared to be toying with these creatures. The inspector either had balls of steel, or he knew these wolfen—perhaps both.

Swoonworthy either way.

"Fuck that actor with his poncy ways and girly clothes—" The big oaf stepped forward in a threatening manner.

"Watch yourself, Conall. Must I remind you this is Abelseth son of Aethelwulf?"

The inspector turned toward the handsome, well-groomed man. "Thank you, cousin, for reminding everyone who I am, but I'm afraid the young lady and I must be on our way."

Even though her eyes had already seen the truth of the matter, Elle could hardly believe her ears. Inspector Durant was one of them.

He raised the sword and swung the weapon overhead.

The blade turned slowly at first, then quickly gathered speed. Within seconds the hall vibrated from the crushing roar of the wind storm. Chairs fell over. Tables slid. Carpets rolled. Tapestries thrashed about before being ripped off rods. The powerful vortex flung her abductors to the far corners of the room. Bones crunched and skulls cracked as they bounced off stone walls and onto bare floors.

The inspector grabbed hold of her hand as he addressed the pile of furniture and dazed men. "Terribly rude of us to dash off without tidying up, but—"

Elle's stomach did somersaults as she was whisked

off in a cyclone of fairy dust and blurred images.

*

"Listen to my voice. Slow deep breaths, that's it—" Abelseth used a soft, reassuring voice. At the moment, Elle appeared to be more concerned about catching her breath than she was fearful.

She squeezed his hand as she gasped for air. It took time to learn how to ride the currents of time-space. Newbies always thought they were starved for oxygen, even though they weren't.

"A few more breaths, in and out slowly." He held her close, but not too close. The more he sparked to her pheromones, the more difficult it would be to let her go.

Still, he rubbed her back lightly.

She wore a leather motorcycle jacket over a skimpy slip of a dress. Shimmery stockings ended provocatively shy of her dress hem. And those black suede ankle boots made shapely legs look a mile long.

Beautiful girl. Stunning outfit. Wild lovemaking.

Abelseth shook off the Elle effect. "Better now?"

Her eyebrows squiggled upward, as she searched his face for answers. "What just happened?"

"One of the side effects of the drift is the sensation of not being able to breathe." He was not surprised to see a frown appear. His confirmation of their trip through four dimensional space likely raised more questions than provided answers. And he sensed the typical muddling of the truth was not going to work with this female.

His gaze met smoke-green eyes seeking real answers, not vagaries. He tried to lighten her mood. "Quite a handy way to travel, once you get used to it."

She stared at him. "What are you, Inspector? And who are those men who abducted me?"

Strict rules of secrecy governed all members of the packs. But the rules got sketchier when applied to wolfen outsiders or lone wolves. He would share as much as he could with her, just not tonight.

"All in good time, Ms. Hathaway." A subtle displacement of air caused his nose to twitch. Abelseth sensed…

She read the urgency in his eyes. "They're coming after us, aren't they?"

He nodded. "It will take them a few minutes. They won't pick up our scent right away."

Abelseth surveyed the surroundings. It was nearly impossible to get one's bearings below ground. Danker and darker than the abandoned Shoreditch tube, they'd landed inside one of the subterranean rivers. Mile after mile of ornate brickwork formed waterways that flowed beneath London. "I believe this is River Walbrook. Shall we push on?"

She nodded.

They were able to jog alongside the waterway for some distance, until the tunnel separated into two passages. If he recalled the underground maps correctly, one side likely carried sewage, the other emptied into a nearby basin.

"Which way, Inspector?"

"What does your nose tell you, Ms. Hathaway?"

Her gaze locked on the diverging river ahead, while his fastened on her lower lip, which she caught between her teeth. A nervous habit he found immensely stimulating.

"I believe we should keep to the right."

The ends of his mouth curled. "That is my sense, as well." A howling wind swept down the tunnel. He nodded ahead. "Quickly, now."

They ran until the passage contracted, forcing them onto a narrow ledge beside the rising water. Abelseth reached for her hand. "I'm afraid this may get extremely damp and chilly."

The underground duct continued to narrow and they were soon up to their knees in icy water. He could also sense the wolves closing in, perhaps no more than fifty meters now.

Elle looked back as she waded into stronger currents. "We won't have to swim, will we?" Her brows crashed together. "Can't you just…whoosh us out of here?"

How to explain? "Drift energy is stored energy."

She whirled around. "What are you—recharging?"

At that very moment, the water swelled, lifting them both off the ledge. He reached for her, but her hand slipped from his gasp. "Inspector," she cried, as she was carried off and washed down the slew.

Abelseth swam toward her cries in the dark, hoping to catch her before the current swept her further away. Surfacing for air, he called out to her. "Elle—where are you?"

Tidal rivers could fill these tunnels to the roof

within minutes. Was the Walbrook a tidal river? What did it matter?

"Elle!" he tried again.

"Inspectoooooor!" Her cry for help sputtered over the water's surface.

He reached out to try catch hold of her, but was caught in the same eddy that had carried her away. He sucked in air as he swirled down into the vortex of an oversized drain that emptied him into a larger body of still water.

Inky blackness.

For one terrifying moment, he was down the watery rabbit hole. He could find no reliable up or down, but he also sensed she was close by. He reached out, gave it a good stretch, and touched her hand. Delicate fingers grasped onto his.

A uniform row of lights wavered in the dark. With his lungs near to bursting, he paddled upward. He broke the surface of the pond and pulled Elle up beside him. Gasping for air, she held onto his jacket lapels as he hauled her into his arms. "I've got you."

A few hard kicks were enough to get them close to the edge of the basin. He drew on his last reserve of wolfen strength and tossed her onto the concrete embankment. The sound of her coughing fit was actually reassuring.

These flood control ponds typically had a landing of some kind. He searched for steps and found none. He was about to launch himself up beside Elle when he was lifted into the air and dropped at the feet of several tall wolfen males.

He squinted up at the looming figures. "Maccon?"

"Good to see you again, Abby." His brother stood with his arms crossed over his chest looking like the wolf lord he was.

Abelseth sat up. "Where are we?" He reached for the shivering girl.

"A basin off Regent's canal," his brother answered.

Abelseth studied the men surrounding his brother, not a familiar face in the lot. "And that large swell, the one that washed us into the basin—your doing I suppose."

"Her abductors were close. I couldn't very well abandon my brother in his hour of need, now could I?"

He resisted a bitter retort to his sibling's dig. Instead, he focused on the young woman in his arms. Her skin was pale and her teeth chattered, but she appeared otherwise unharmed.

He gently brushed damp strands of hair off her face. "Feeling well enough?"

Between shivers, she made a fist and raised her thumb.

Maccon squatted beside them. "Beautiful creature." He offered Elle a flask. "A little something to take the chill off."

"I'm not a creature," she coughed up a growl. "I'm a badass…botanist."

Abelseth admired her pluck, but checked his grin. "She's in shock. She's made three trips into the drift tonight, the last one in water, no thanks to you." He rose to his feet with Elle in his arms. "Kindly point us in the direction of her car. I wish to see the young lady home."

Maccon handed Elle his flask. "Drink—it will warm you up."

Elle took small sips and returned the flask. "Thank you," she croaked softly.

His brother frowned. "You'll need an escort."

Abelseth returned an icier frown. "That won't be necessary."

"A precaution. Let us help you, Abby." His brother backed off and led the way. They kept to the canal towpath and then side streets until they arrived in the alley where he'd parked Elle's Mini Cooper.

"Good God—car keys." Abelseth set Elle down and searched his pockets. For a tense moment, he pictured the small cluster of metal objects settled into the muddy bottom of the basin. "Ah-ha!" His fingers hooked into the ring, and retrieved her keys. "A small, yet significant tragedy avoided."

Eyes wide and large, she nodded in relief. "There's a football throw in the boot."

While he fetched the blanket, Elle peeled off a sopping wet jacket.

She rather pointedly gazed back at Maccon and his men. "Stay where you are—behind the car."

Abelseth shook the blanket out.

"Hold it behind me, please?" The young lady boldly shrugged out of thin straps and the dress slipped to the ground.

Too late to turn away.

The briefest, most transparent thong wrapped over her hips, and no bra. Lovely breasts with blush colored nipples set high on the curve—erect and inviting. Gorgeous, all parts of her.

She even managed a sly smile. "Wrap me up?"

"Yes, of course." He cocooned her in warm fleece and tucked her inside the car.

Lucy stirred in the backseat. "About time you two showed up."

"I'm afraid this evening's been a bit of a damp squib—" Abelseth thought better of making light of Elle's abduction and near drowning. "Never mind." He closed the door and circled round to the driver's side.

Maccon leaned against the car blocking the door. "Pretty girl. And her wolf is showing—does she know it?"

"Why the interest, Maccon? In Ms. Hathaway. In me." He tossed damp strands of hair off his face. "What's going on?"

Maccon shrugged. "This was likely Exers' doing, they're on the prowl of late."

He found his brother's reference to the rebel pack disturbing. In fact, he wondered how close the Lords and Exers had become in his absence.

Abelseth cursed under his breath. "They abducted Elle off the street, in front of XOYO."

His brother's frown deepened.

"To be fair, they weren't all Exers." They both pivoted toward the voice behind them.

Phelan sauntered forward. "This was more of a freelance job, using bachelors from several packs."

Abelseth's gaze moved between his cousin and brother. "Might I ask what you were doing in that meeting room, Phelan?"

"Hanging with the insurgents. They're outlaws,

cuz—most of the local packs won't have—"

Lucy powered down the window. "Us working girls need our beauty sleep, Inspector."

"Come to dinner tomorrow evening," Maccon urged him. "My place, seven sharp."

He must have scowled, because his brother softened his order. "Izzy will be over the moon to see you. Give us another chance, Abelseth." The leader of the Lords pivoted, then turned back. "Bring the female, if you wish."

Abelseth backed the Mini out of the alley and headed south.

Lucy edged up between them. "Nice looking blokes, who were they?" She studied them both with interest. "And why are you both sopping?"

Elle stared daggers at him. "Yes, why exactly are we sopping wet, Inspector Durant?"

He mumbled something about slipping into the river and out of the clutches of street gangs. "Where shall I drop you, Lucy?"

"Sixteen Artillery Lane, Spitalfields. I share a flat above The Mayor of Scaredy Cat Town." Relieved to change the subject, he made small talk. "Must be noisy living above a trendy cocktail bar."

"Lively as well as convenient. I work there on weekends." Lucy went right back to the blokes in the alley. "A bit posh for street thugs, wouldn't you say, Inspector?"

He braked for a traffic light. "There are gangs. And then there are the gangsters who run them." He spent the rest of the trip feigning ignorance and muddling with the truth. "Perhaps you might ask Elle about this evening's events in the morning?"

He turned down a narrow alley and stopped in the middle of the row. Elle had quietly endured the ride, and as the car warmed, her cheeks took on a rosy glow.

"You all right, Elle?" Lucy asked, as she climbed out of the car.

"I'll be fine—see you bright and early."

"Double cappuccino, double sugar, plenty of foam." Lucy winked. "Sleep tight, you two."

Abelseth drove for several blocks in silence. He checked the heater. "Too warm? Not warm enough?" Minutes dragged on without a word.

Finally, she spoke. "Was this night, in fact, about me or you, Inspector?"

In the bright light of Piccadilly Circus, Elle's fierce gaze was pure wolfen female. Better than tears, he supposed. "Any guess on my part would be premature, though I suspect your abductor's interest has more to do with you, Ms. Hathaway."

"When we were swept up by the river you called me Elle—call me Elle, please." She was sending mixed messages. One minute happy to disrobe in front of him, the next fiercely pugnacious. "Take Bishopsgate to Upper Thames, you'll save two minutes."

"As you wish, Elle." His lips pressed together flatlined in defeat. The fact that she wanted to shave two minutes off the drive said it all. He'd blown his chances with the petulant young beauty.

He pulled into the mews off Chester Street.

"Three doors down on the left." Elle reached

up, pressed a button on the visor and a garage door opened.

He parked the car and killed the engine.

She stared straight ahead. "What could they possibly want with me?"

He sensed the wary wolf in her nature, the part of her who'd been taught never to reveal herself. "Elle...I cannot answer honestly if you cannot be honest with me."

She pressed the latch. He helped her gather her things, and unlocked the door that led upstairs to her flat. He handed over keys, stockings, shoes and dress, leaving the shriveled leather jacket for last.

"Wicked jacket."

"Used to be." She tossed the soggy garment inside and the blanket loosened, creating a mesmerizing wardrobe malfunction.

He pointed to a perky, translucent-pink nipple. "Your throw has slipped."

She made no move to cover herself. She simply stepped back and slammed the door in his face.

Chapter

SIX

Confessions of a werewolf.

Elle tapped the snooze button on her phone and pulled the duvet up to her chin. The pleasant drum of rain on pavers drifted into her bedroom from the alley below. Farther away, the splash of car tires, and the blare of a car horn on Upper Belgrave Street.

She cracked an eye open. Meandering water droplets spotted the window panes. Her nose twitched. Top notes of asphalt and ozone, the scent of city rain. Hints of black tea and—she sniffed again—burnt crumpets. Her neighbor still didn't have a feel for his new Dualit toaster.

Barely awake, and she was already on sensory overload.

She reached for her phone on the nightstand. Seven forty-three. It took twenty minutes to shower, pull on leggings, a tee shirt, boyfriend sweater and rain boots. She'd drive the Mini to work today, which made her commute no more than ten minutes.

That gave her some time to ponder. Five minutes to try and make sense of last night. And ten minutes to contemplate Detective Inspector Durant.

She should be worried. A day off the suppressant

and she'd been abducted, and for no good reason. Mother had cautioned her for years that fully engaged werewolves had extraordinary abilities, sensory and otherwise. She also strongly suspected her mother had withheld things, information she could use right now.

Not a soul in London knew she was wolf-blooded, except for Iggy Binns, her supplier of lycosopene. Oddly, he'd once called her his most valuable client. She'd ignored his remark, thought it to be a flirtation, but now she wished she'd pressed him for an explanation.

Elle chewed her bottom lip. Who else might know her secret? There was a chance Julian suspected something. And Tom Wells, the director of Chelsea Physic Garden. During her job interview, he'd mentioned that he knew her mother, but she hadn't followed up on his remark. There it was again—popping up its ugly head—the long ingrained fear of exposing either herself or her mother. And to make matters worse, her evasion might have given her away, revealed her nature to a clan or pack she knew nothing about.

How awful, now she was worried about being too fearful. Elle dove under the covers and moved onto another worrisome subject. Inspector Durant, wolf detective.

He knew she was a latent female. She was absolutely sure of it. And his call for mutual honesty had challenged, as well as thrilled her. She replayed snippets of last night's adventures in her head. The crowded dance floor at XOYO. The devilish handsome Inspector had appeared in front of her. Tall and virile and strong, with those crystalline blue eyes that glimmered under the swirling lights.

He'd startled her at first, and then he'd gently ravaged her lips with his mouth. And his teeth.

A shot of arousal tingled through her body. Moaning softly, she tossed off the covers. Everything after that electrifying kiss was a blur. Elle sat on the edge of the bed and stared at her feet. Absently, she wiggled painted toenails—a vibrant shade of lilac called *Bodacious*.

She'd been abducted, rescued and nearly drowned. And it all seemed so thrilling. It was as if she'd dreamed last night, or experienced some form of delirium. Add to that the itchy feeling of wanting to shiver out her own skin. Without her daily fix, her wolf senses were becoming more acute. And as her dual nature emerged, there would other issues—like those strange new lycanthrope powers.

Elle padded across the cold wood floor to the bath and medicine cabinet. She checked all three stashes, ending with the tampon box. She dumped a half dozen paper covered tubes out, hoping to find a stray capsule.

Crappola. Nothing.

She did a double take in the mirror—eyes large and agitated, pale complexion. Nothing a bit of rosy glow blush wouldn't cover. She substituted two aspirin for her meds and stepped into the shower.

Hot and steamy, just like Inspector Durant.

*

Abelseth dodged a bit of street traffic as he headed for the stately shopfront on the corner of Savile Row. At the top of the entry stairs, he paused at the door and tried to shake off the after effect of her. He concentrated on the names engraved on the polished brass door plaque: Gieves & Hawkes, Bespoke Tailor.

He continued to stare, hoping to chase lustful thoughts away. Any moment now, his morning double shot of espresso would kick in and erase the picture of Elle dancing under a swirl of flashing light, hips swaying, hair flying around her beautiful face. And later, wrapping that breathtaking body in a Chelsea Football Club blanket.

A Bentley pulled up in front of the shop entrance. Abelseth pivoted as the rear passenger door opened. He half expected Prince Charles or Sir Elton John to exit the long black car.

Instead, the door remained open.

Abelseth stepped back onto the street and dipped down for a look. Hawkish, beady eyes returned his gaze. The silver haired gentleman inside the vehicle was all too familiar.

"Lord Severn, what brings you to town? A fitting, perhaps?"

"Get in Abelseth, and do call me Uncle."

He climbed in beside his relative, and tried to remember the last time he'd seen or spoken to Algernon de Vere, Earl of Wessex, Viscount Severn.

The limo sped down the lane of luxury menswear shops and turned onto Regent Street. An oozer of urbane sophistication, Uncle had not had changed much these past five years. Reading spectacles now perched on the end of a thin straight nose. Hair a bit more silver than black.

Methodically, he put away the brief he'd been reading and folded his glasses. "You're looking windblown and disheveled…" Steely gray eyes trailed up and down his person. "As usual."

"Some things never change, isn't that right, Uncle?"

After a brief exchange of cool assessments and strained pleasantries, Abelseth grew impatient. "Since this is not a chance encounter, I expect there must be a reason for this sojourn…?"

Pale eyes narrowed. "The dead man you're investigating is a middleman for an as yet unknown chemist entrepreneur. The distributor's full name is Ignatius Binns, goes by the handle—Iggy."

Abelseth frowned. "Am I to assume you have clearance to go poking about in my cases?"

His uncle shrugged. "I chair a special committee on homeland security. How difficult could it be?" The elder man angled toward him for a second uncomfortable inspection.

"Mind telling me what's going on, Uncle?"

"The bloodlines are weak, it's happening in all the clans. Too many made wolves, not enough native blood."

"And whose fault is that, Uncle?"

"No doubt we scared the females off—forced mating contracts and the like."

"And the like." Abelseth snorted softly. "How kind we are to ourselves."

His uncle ignored the remark. "The mauled dealer found in the tube station made himself a small fortune selling the lycanthrope suppressant, lycosopene, to a very exclusive female clientele." His uncle rattled on, "Extremely cunning. Took us years to find him."

Abelseth stared. "You had him murdered."

Shrewd wolfen eyes narrowed slightly. "I do not bully. I do not order. I merely suggest." His stare lingered uncomfortably. "Don't look so glum, murder was never my intention. We were after his source—the maker of this *ly-cos-o-pene...*" Uncle emphasized each syllable, hissing the name like it was snake venom. "Nevertheless, we got him, and none too soon. The barbarians are at the gate, my boy."

Lord Severn no doubt referred to Ex Cereberus—the insurgent pack who'd attempted to abduct Elle last night.

"Bloody renegade wolves." Uncle shook his head. "We knew this was coming, now they're strong, surprisingly well-educated, and ready to rule."

As a young wolf, his uncle had taught him to never to look away from any man or wolf he didn't trust. Besides being excellent advice, the irony was near breathtaking at the moment.

Abelseth frowned. "I suppose you want me to cover up any hints of wolfen involvement."

"In two days' time, a pack of dead street dogs will be found in one of the Piccadilly Line tunnels. *Homicidium enigma terminatum.*"

"Case closed. You think of everything, Uncle." On some level, one had to admire the intestinal fortitude it took to make a murder look like an unfortunate mauling.

"Not quite, Abelseth. There is a brilliant chemist out there who designed the suppressant. All I have is a name—Sloane Mars."

Abelseth stared at his uncle. "You want me to find this chemist before the other packs do."

"Our line grows weaker by the year. We held a council recently and voted. Only pure-blooded mates—no more made females. Ask your brother about Isolde. There have been difficulties."

Childbirth for made females was not without risk to both mother and newborn. And there were no guarantees that offspring would turn. Half-blooded cubs, it was argued, were physically weaker and often times harder to train in the transmutational arts.

Pure blooded females were not only rare, they were difficult to meet these days. Many of them had been hidden away as girls and told terrifying, lurid stories. And then came the lycan suppressant, which had improved over the years with fewer side effects. Pre-pubescent, pure-blooded girls were routinely started on lycosopene. Without the drug in their system, these females would become infinitely easier to track and locate.

Abelseth exhaled a harsh sigh. Five years ago, he'd left his pack angry, but not so angry that he didn't respect many aspects of the culture he'd been raised in. For a fleeting moment, he wanted to chuck it all, move back to Essex and deny his wolf legacy.

He dismissed the thought out of hand.

Walking away wasn't the solution. He'd tried to

isolate himself, only to return again. And though he still felt a considerable amount of ambivalence toward his pack, his re-indoctrination felt inevitable. There was also another beautiful, slam-the-door-in-his-face reason for remaining in London.

The limousine pulled curbside at the south end of Westminster Palace. "Right, I've given you a name, and I understand there is a witness, a suppressant user. I expect weekly reports." His uncle reached for a slim leather portfolio. "The young female you rescued last night—your witness. What do you know about her?"

Abelseth sensed his uncle's casual aside masked a keen interest in Elle.

"She's an innocent. As a favor to me, leave her out of this."

The gleam in Lord Severn's eyes flickered before fading. "For now."

Chapter

SEVEN

A lovely night for a moondance with Elle.

Abelseth landed on the roof of the Embassy of the Republic of Côte d'Ivoire. From there, he had a clear view of Elle's apartment, along with Belgravia and Knightsbridge beyond. As twilight faded, the myriad of lights that adorned Harrods department store twinkled to life.

He lowered himself onto his haunches.

Elle hurriedly packed a carry-on bag, locked up the flat and tossed the overnighter into the boot of her car. A last-minute getaway of some kind, and not a bad idea under the circumstances. He watched her traverse the mews and disappear into a stately residence, reappearing a few minutes later on the roof garden terrace. She appeared to be giving the hot house a look-over, checking thermostats, watering systems, automatic timers. She flipped a switch and closed the door to the glass house.

A fine mist rained down on the exotic flowering plants. From speakers hidden around the terrace, a soothing rhythm track and breathy female voice floated up into the night air—haunting, seductive, tempting.

Elle turned up the sound system.

He inhaled sharply, enthralled by her silhouette against the glow from a nearby street lamp. With her arms above her head, she wove her hands together then apart—entwined fingers fluttering, re-entwining. Her body swayed, reluctant to move. Then, as if she couldn't resist the music, she moved into a series of lovely turns.

She wore a short, flirty skirt over black leggings. A casual, urban ballerina dancing a fairy waltz. An enchantment one might run across in a magical wood, not the rooftop of a West End palace.

Mesmerized, Abelseth watched her move effortlessly from one set of variations to another, practicing different sequences of steps, some languid and dreamlike, others pixieish and full of clever hops and turns.

His nostrils flared.

He scanned the quiet neighborhood populated by foreign embassies and the stately mansions of the uber-wealthy. A security patrol car turned the corner at Upper Belgrave and traveled north, toward the square.

Wolfen were about.

He made the short jump through the drift, and was careful to be stealthy about it. He landed in a crouched position on the roof garden.

Elle ended her dance with a startled gasp. "Inspector Durant, whatever are you—" Doe-eyed, and more than a little fearful, she shook her head. "You need to stay away, please go."

Abelseth rose slowly and walked toward her.

She backed away. "It's a simple enough requ—"

"You've made that impossible for me." He slipped his hand around her waist, and drew her in.

She pressed her palms against his chest.

He persisted gently and she swayed closer.

"Dance with me, Elle." He turned her in slow circles at first, then faster, until they whirled around the patio in three-four time.

The barest smile crossed her lips. "I thought you didn't dance."

He varied the length of his strides and the speed of his turns, which made it impossible not to appreciate how well they moved together. "I lied."

She arched away, meeting his gaze directly. "You lie about a lot of things, Inspector." She brushed up against him, releasing pheromones—ylang ylang with hints of she-wolf.

"I withhold information for good reason."

Her brows squiggled together. "You lied or obfuscated with every story you told to distract—"

"Something you never do." His mouth twitched.

A sliver of crescent moon glimmered in her eyes.

Quite suddenly, he was willing to take a huge risk. Break all the wolfen rules past, present, and future. Was he under the spell of the new moon or this beautiful girl? Did he care?

He slowed to a near standstill. "Elle…if I confessed to you everything about myself, would you leave the boundaries of your life?"

"I don't…date wolves." She stepped away, tossing long waves of hair over her shoulders, and revealing more of her pale blue cardigan. The cropped sweater exposed a hint of midriff and hugged the curves of her breasts. He had no trouble remembering how lovely she was naked. He'd nearly come undone by her raw beauty.

He needed an enticement of some sort. Something she couldn't resist—something that would buy him enough time to state his case. "I believe you might consider a wolf, after a moondance."

She tilted her head and squinted. "Moondance?"

He stepped back and leapt into the air, gracefully turning an airborne pirouette and landing softly on a ledge above the green house. Before she could catch her breath, he pushed off into the air again, coattails flying—leaping from one rooftop to another, weightlessly tumbling and turning through the air.

The rooftop garden had several terraced levels, one for the glass house, a second for dining and socializing, and yet another for hydrotherapy. Abelseth spiraled downward, landing on the edge of the spa, several feet above her.

"That was...brilliant..." Elle stammered, wide-eyed.

"Dance with me, then."

"But I—" she protested, "I don't believe I can dance in the air."

He dropped down in front of her. "We call it surfing the drift. It feels like you're riding the curves of a wave." He held out his hand. "You are wolf-blooded, Elle, you can do this."

"But, what if I fall?"

"You won't."

Her eyes shimmered with excitement. "Because

you won't let that happen." She walked into his arms.

He drew her in close and lifted off slowly. When they reached the height of the glass house roof, he turned them in circles. "Hold onto my hand." He released her from his arms, and swept her around his body, increasing the speed of her circles, until the stars spun around her head.

He drew her back in. "That was lovely," Elle whispered.

"To connect with the drift, you reach out from your solar plexus. I can't explain how you do this, but you will know. Don't overthink it, just—"

They were suddenly thrown higher up into the air, well above the rooftops. Her eyes grew wide, and slightly panicked. "My word—was that me? Am I doing this?"

They fell to earth suddenly and Abelseth slowed their decent. He chuckled softly, and the dear girl laughed as well.

Music swelled up into the night air from the garden below. "Once more, Elle—only this time, follow my lead."

Without letting go entirely, he encouraged her to whirl up into the air, giving her a boost now and then, to help keep her aloft.

"It's as if I'm floating on a cushion of air or a breeze." Before he could stop her, Elle tried a pirouette.

Reach out from your center. He felt her lock into the drift, then just as quickly she lost it and plunged toward the ground. He swooped down and caught her, landing them safely back on the terrace.

"You have a brave heart. Why do you hide it, Elle?"

She stepped away and he pulled her back, capturing her mouth under his, parting those pouty lips. His tongue plunged in deep—chasing, teasing, purposely arousing her.

Find your wild, Elle.

Sensing the quickening of her pulse, he pushed off into the drift, pressing her against the wall of the manse. He thrust against the heat of her body, and she answered with her hips, flinging them across the garden. More breathless kissing, even some hot, sexy laughter as they crashed into an ivy-covered privacy fence.

"Rough foreplay in the space-time continuum is a favorite of mine." He swept both hands under her skirt and she wrapped her legs around him. Consumed by lust, he barely noticed the subtle shift of shadow and light. Not until unfamiliar pheromones assaulted his nose—wolves on the hunt—did he come up for air.

He brushed his lips over her neck and cheek. "Stay right where you are. I shall return shortly."

He took a step back before vaulting over the rooftop and landing in the narrow lane below. Elle peeked over the top of the privacy wall. The girl was incorrigible. Still, he smiled. She appeared to be using the drift with a good measure of control.

He placed a finger to his lips. *Not a peep, Elle.*

Rising from his haunches, he moved down the alley, avoiding porch lights, darting in and out of doorways.

One of the packs had picked up Elle's scent.

There—just ahead, several wolfen circled the Horse and Groom, a neighborhood pub tucked into a corner of the mews.

He could hear snippets of conversation. Enough to know these wolves were after Elle and that they knew they were close. Bugger! It was all that moondancing and lust. He and Elle might have just as well sent up flares.

Abelseth faded back down the alley and returned to Elle. The slower his exit and reentry the better, he'd barely leave a whisper in the drift.

He stepped out of the shadows. "I presume you were about to leave town? Visit a friend or relation?" He scanned the roof garden. "Elle?"

Hurried footsteps came from inside the residence. He caught her at the bottom of the servants' stairs. Turning her around, he searched her face—honest, open, frightened.

"You're making a run for it." He delved in deep, trying to read her. She backed off and he grabbed hold of her. "And you're searching for answers."

"I can do this on my own."

Bloody mad of her to try and go it alone. "You're fearless, but you're also acting foolishly, Elle. Let me distract them, enough to get you out of the mews and on your way."

She tried wriggling out of his grip, but the moment their gazes met her defiance waned. After a few deep breaths, she nodded.

Abelseth cracked the door and searched the far end of the mews. "Three wolfen have staked out the pub." He checked her garage. "Stroke of luck, you left the garage door open and porch light off."

Elle set the alarm in the manse and stepped out into the alley. He nodded for her to go, and they made a run for the garage.

He held the door and she tucked herself into the car. "Exit onto Chester Street and make as little noise as possible until you're well away. Do not stop for any reason—that means stop signs, traffic lights and wolves."

He pushed the Mini out of the garage and down the lane. The second she turned the ignition key, he jumped in and out of the drift.

"Any sign of her?" Abelseth stepped out of the pub door. He easily read the raised brows and sullen looks of the competing pack members. "I wager she's somewhere in the nearabout—have any of you picked up her scent?"

Snarling wolves chased him out of the mews. He led them down Chapel Street, toward Grosvenor Place, and away from Elle. Deep into Green Park, he vanished from sight.

He sensed many things about Elle, in particular, she was a Wessex girl through and through. Her fresh-faced beauty, and direct way of speaking had been his first clue.

Abelseth pictured the quickest route out of town, exiting and reentering the drift, sending feelers out. On his third jump he spotted the orange Mini Cooper with the racing stripe. But the rogue pack had caught his drift and were not far behind.

Elle stopped for a traffic light.

A leering bearded male, with fiery eyes

materialized in the seat beside her.

"No-oooo!" Abelseth dove for the door, ripped the wolf out of her car and sent him flying into the drift.

He settled in beside her and calmly raised the window.

For a split second, Elle stared open-mouthed, then floored the accelerator. "Who was that?"

"I believe he's Ex Cereberus—we call them Exers. Lone wolves mostly, who left their packs years ago." He refrained from telling her the full story. In truth, they'd been cast out for a number of nefarious deeds, including their ruthless abduction of young females.

He quieted the snarl in his voice. "Keep to your right and take the Waterloo Bridge."

Elle turned south, tires squealing. She checked her rearview mirror.

Well aware of the blurred shapes and elusive shadows leaping in and out of sight behind the car, he sensed Elle had also caught a glimpse of them in flux. Half wolves, half men, as they rebounded through the toroidal fields in pursuit of her.

"It's called whipping the drift—very dangerous— fractal patterns get jumbled. If you're too far off…" He shook his head. "…there's no way to put Humpty Dumpty back together again."

One of the Exers materialized in front of the car, and Elle hit the brake pedal.

"Do not slow down, head straight for him."

"But—"

"Trust me."

She braced herself behind the steering wheel and blew through the creature—or the vapor that had once been a wolfman.

"You see? Nobody lying in the street. Not a scratch to the grille."

She darted a glance his way. "Don't make me do that again."

"Faster the better—make it hard for them."

Elle drove like a mad demon, accelerating well beyond posted limits, blowing through roundabouts, snaking in and out of traffic, sliding through turns…

He grabbed the roof handle. "Where'd you learn to do that?"

She shook her head. "I have no idea."

Elle burned up the road, putting them well ahead of the pack, and they made it across the river without further incident.

"For the record, this new wolfy part of me sucks." She briefly consulted the GPS monitor on the dash. "Which way, now?"

His lips twitched. "Two lefts—Stamford then Duchy."

She darted squinty-eyes at him. "Do you find my discomfort amusing?"

"Not in the least, in fact, I can relate."

Her gaze softened. "Sorry, being chased by rabid wolves makes me peevish."

In his attempt to suppress a laugh, he snickered a bit.

"Will you stop—what did I do now?"

"Nothing. It's just that I've never heard anyone use the word peevish, at least not in this century."

She cranked the steering wheel and the Mini deftly made the turn onto Stamford. "Mind telling me where we're going?"

"That imposing new high-rise just ahead, past the OXO Tower."

"Of course I'm happy to drop you off..." Elle leaned forward and looked both ways before running the traffic light. "...before I leave town."

"My brother is having a dinner party. We'll be surrounded by my pack."

She slid into a parking space on Duchy Street and turned to him. "Inspector Durant, are you inviting me to a party?"

"At the moment, the safest place for you to be is among wolves."

Chapter

EIGHT

A dinner party where Elle is the featured dish.

"But—I'm not dressed for a dinner party," Elle protested.

There were times, when his gaze alone captured her completely. "You look beautiful just the way you are, in leggings and that flirty mini skirt." Long lashes shaded his crystalline eyes, which lowered to the v-neckline of her cardigan. "You've left your sweater unbuttoned, enough to reveal an alluring hollow between the curves of your breasts. And when you exhale, a hint of flesh."

Elle sucked in a breath. She was neither well-endowed nor small-breasted, but the glimmer in his eyes told her she was just right.

His gaze slowly traveled upward, through rebellious waves of hair she had little control over. "If I dare mention your effortless sense of style, you'll have a laugh—dismiss me outright."

"I would never do that." She tried hard not to grin and failed.

He snorted a laugh at himself. "You look lovely. And this isn't a formal dinner party."

Something intimate was happening between them.

They were bickering with a good deal of eye contact. Quarreling lovers who might have a quick boff in the car before the party. The she-wolf in her wanted to feel his lips on hers, the scrape of his teeth across her breast, his hard thrust into her body...

Abelseth reached over and killed the engine, along with her fantasy. "I really must insist, Elle, for your safety."

A wisp of fog rolled off the Thames and crept up the lane. He was offering her his protection, as well as an introduction to his pack. It was the smart move, she supposed. "One hour—then I'm off."

He hustled her into the building, and past security. The lobby of the South Tower was elegant and modern, yet she barely noticed the abstract art and minimalist furnishings.

"What am I to call you? Abelseth? Abby?" She waited for the brow arch, which came predictably, although not quite as pronounced as yesterday.

"I prefer Abelseth."

Red LED letters crawled across the top of the sleek metal lift doors. Intensely aware of the man standing beside her, she concentrated on the time and temperature compliments of Lloyd's Bank. "Your brother calls you Abby. Is that because he wants to provoke you?"

"I'm afraid it's a family sobriquet, part affection, part needling."

"Sobriquet," she mused aloud. "Is that one of your Scrabble words?"

She caught the tail end of a grin. He wore that fleeting, sexy smile so well it annoyed her. Mostly because it made her heart race and her body shiver. She exhaled a sigh. "I shall call you Abby or Abelseth...depending."

His gaze drilled into her. "On?"

"My mood, your temperament." She toyed with the tassel on her boho shoulder bag. "If we're getting on or not—various circumstances."

The doors opened with a ding and he followed her into the lift. "Ah—like mother."

Hyperaware of his proximity, she watched him slide a security card into a slot beside the floor buttons. When the red light flashed green, he punched numbers onto an adjacent keypad.

"Complicated," she murmured as the doors closed.

"Centuries ago we used drawbridges and moats, today it's magnetic cards and passwords."

Her knees suddenly went wobbly and her stomach fell. She blamed the queer sensation on the rising lift, not his piercing gaze. Elle exhaled a sigh. This was all so deliciously taboo.

The man standing beside her was not just wolfen. He was significant to a pack with powerful affiliations. She should be wary and yet she was drawn to him. A wild thing she barely knew writhed beneath her skin, aching to know him in ways that set her cheeks on fire. There were times when she couldn't trust this new mysterious creature around him.

He moved closer, but did not touch her. The warmth of his breath brushed the side of her neck. "Elle—"

She turned and pressed her lips to his, delivering a kiss so deep and raw, she shocked even herself. And she opened to him, curling her tongue over and under his.

Abelseth returned her kiss with a fierce, tender passion that sent shivers through all her girl parts. Soft and sensual, with an occasional playful bite or scrape of his teeth. For the first time in her life she was experiencing the full meaning of the words arousal and desire—impulses that made her whimper as his tongue plundered and explored.

And there were darker urges. She wanted to do things with him. Naughty things she'd either avoided or pushed away in her short, uneventful life.

Until now.

"I want to experience your wolf," he whispered in her ear. "Nuzzle the ruff of your coat." Pliant, sensuous lips brushed her neck. "Feast on your scent. Bite you…" He nipped her earlobe. "…In places you can't even imagine."

A wicked surge of wolf lust rippled through her body. Lost in the heat of his words, Elle barely noticed the lift doors open.

He broke off their kiss, but held her close. "You're trembling."

"All your fault, Abelseth." Her words buffeted gently off his lips.

A cough, a bit of throat clearing and a few titters permeated her consciousness.

Those gorgeous eyes of his crinkled. "I'm afraid this lift opens directly onto the apartment."

They turned in unison.

A number of people, men mostly, stood in the foyer. Facial expressions ran from quizzical brows to mild amusement to salacious grins. Elle recognized the attractive gang leader from the previous evening. The very same man who'd offered her a nip from his flask.

"Welcome, brother."

Abelseth greeted his sibling as they stepped out of the lift. "Good evening, Maccon."

Their host wore a black on black pinstripe suit with a crisp white shirt and charcoal tie, all of it tailored to perfection. He pivoted toward her. "And the lovely Ms...?"

Abelseth made formal introductions. "Elle Hathaway, my brother Maccon Durant."

Dark eyes slid down the buttons of her sweater. "Pretty name—just like the girl. Lovely to see you both."

A hush fell over the room as guests whispered amongst themselves. Necks craned and bodies pivoted to try and catch a glimpse of them.

She edged closer. "Everyone is dressed, you said—"

Abelseth kissed her hard and possessively. "You don't need a cocktail dress, Elle, they're all mesmerized by you."

A stunning young woman in a body-hugging sheath eased up beside Abelseth and helped him shrug out of his top coat. "I see you finally got 'round for a visit," she teased, tilting her head.

Abelseth turned toward the attractive female. "Had to get it over with sooner or later."

Her eyes drank him in. "Try to be civil, Abby, things have changed. The pack needs you—I need you." She kissed him on the mouth briefly.

She turned and smiled at Elle, while giving her the once over. "I'm Isolde, but everyone calls me Izzy." Abelseth introduced Elle to the raven-haired seductress, who turned out to be his brother's mate.

"You both look like you could use a relaxer." Maccon's gaze shifted to Izzy. "Right, luv?"

The seductive young woman tucked her arm through Abelseth's. "Come, let's get you both a drink." She glanced back at Elle. "We're at least two good stiff ones ahead of you. You must catch up."

Maccon placed his hand at the small of Elle's back and steered her though the crowded room. By the time they arrived at the bar, she'd been introduced to nearly everyone at the party.

There was an air of eminence about the brothers, especially here, in this posh flat with members of their pack surrounding them. Maccon came off as urbane, polished, with a charming relaxed manner about him. What surprised Elle more was the reaction to her date.

Abelseth's ancient wolf-prince had emerged, in all of its quiet strength and grace. And seeing him interact with his pack, was intriguing. Many of them appeared to be enamored—of him? by him? for him? She wondered. There was no shortage of head dips and subtle bows whenever he greeted one of them.

"What's your poison, Elle?" Maccon asked.

"A glass of Chardonnay, please."

While she sipped the fruity wine, Abelseth nursed a single malt whiskey and spoke in low tones with his sibling. "Exers again tonight. Elle was on her way out of town. We dropped in here to wait them out."

Maccon snorted a laugh. "And here Izzy and I thought you actually missed us."

"Absolutely true, I've missed you both." He reached out to her and Elle slipped her hand in his. She noted his brother's skeptical eyebrow. Every bit as severe as an Abelseth arch, though not as eloquent.

Maccon knocked back half his drink. "Exers have become a nuisance, what with the purge on."

Abelseth snorted a laugh. "Purge, is that what you're calling it?"

Elle peered over his shoulder. Maccon's vivacious mate chatted up a few friends standing near the bar. Briefly, the attractive female returned her gaze.

Truth be told, Elle was intrigued. What might it be like to be the mate of a dishy powerful pack leader? Have oodles of money, live in a penthouse and throw lavish dinner parties?

Who was she kidding, she'd suck at it.

Elle returned to the two brothers' conversation. Maccon was saying something about a quick counsel. "I'll round up a few advisors, back in a flash."

The moment his brother excused himself, Abelseth pulled her into a quiet niche. "I'm not sure how to put this, but the more people believe we're—"

"Mated?"

He nodded. "The safer you'll be." Since their arrival, several young males had eyed her continuously. Her date had met their gazes with a silent warning. *Do not dare touch her*. Or a something to that effect.

Elle sighed. "You don't trust your own pack?"

"I trust no one."

Elle snuggled against him. "I'm curious about Izzy."

"Never mind her, she kisses everyone."

She leaned back and made eye contact. "Not the kiss, it's the way she stares at you when you're not looking."

"I see." He wagged his head a bit. Contemplating a lie, perhaps?

"Is it really that difficult to explain, Abelseth?"

"So it's to be Abelseth when I'm testing your patience."

"Is it really so difficult to explain—Abby?" She taunted him with a lip curl. "Better?"

He exhaled a masculine sigh of surrender. "Izzy was with me before she was with my brother. We never formally mated."

"Plenty of informal mating, I imagine." She gulped pale gold liquid.

He stared at her. "Five years ago, Maccon stole her away and made her. I took it rather hard at the time. Gave up the Lords, moved away, became an officer of the law."

Elle gazed around the room. "You also became a legend...of sorts."

"The pack has romanticized the story."

"I imagine they begged you to come back."

Abelseth shrugged. "It took them awhile to find me. Their calls and letters stopped after a few years." His gaze swept over her features—eyes, tip of the nose, a curve of cheek, he paused at her lips. "It all seems foolish and overwrought now." No man had ever looked at her in this way. As if he needed to possess her, ravage her, protect her.

"I imagine that wolfy look works on most girls," she stated softly. "Do you cultivate that sexy stare, the one that says 'I want to tear off that pretty little frock, and go down on you?'"

She moved away, and he pulled her back. "What works on you, Elle?"

The truth of the matter? Everything about him worked on her. He possessed the strength of ten men, in character as well as in might. She revisited the dizzying, dream-like experience of drifting with him under a crescent moon. And those dazzling eyes, difficult to meet directly, even harder to break away from.

Smooth background jazz segued into a smoky saxophone. The kind of music that encourages the rapid removal of clothes—if they were lovers, and alone.

Drawing her close, his breath ruffled the wisps of hair at her temple. His affection felt genuine, yet she was well aware of the purpose behind this lovely snog. He was sending a clear signal to his pack by marking her as his.

And he played his role with conviction. Sheltering, and protective, with a powerful shot of alpha male sex appeal. She couldn't stop—didn't even try to stop—the shower of tingles that rippled through her body.

She should be wary but she wasn't. She was drawn to him, like no man she had ever been with. Raging pheromones danced between them, telegraphing their desire. The entire dinner party sensed it.

"Are you always this intimate with your dates?"

He nuzzled her cheek and ear. "Never."

Elle sucked in a breath and reminded herself that the uber-hot, self-possessed detective also had fangs and claws.

"Ah, Miss Hathaway." They both turned toward the sleek, silver-haired gentleman closing in on them. "And Abelseth, delighted to see you again."

Elle shivered a bit. "You know my name—have we met before?" She turned to Abelseth. "I don't understand."

"My dear, your stellar reputation proceeds you." Refined in appearance and impeccably dressed, the man gave her a flagrant once-over.

"Elle, this my uncle, Algernon de Vere, Earl of Wessex, Viscount Severn."

She nodded. "Lord Severn."

"At last we meet." Liquid black pupils darkened steel-gray eyes that penetrated. Instinctively, she quieted her thoughts.

A few more pack members approached in rapid succession. Maccon leaned in. "Sorry to interrupt— may I steal Abby away for a brief consult?"

Abelseth cocked his brow a bit. "You don't mind?" He backed away.

"Go—" Elle plastered a smile on her face and returned to Lord Severn.

"Top up?" he asked.

She held up her near empty glass. "Please."

The silver-haired gentleman escorted her to the bar. "I'm afraid that lovely Chardonnay is gone, but

206

all is not lost." He raised a bottle of champagne and squinted at the label. "Ruinart Blanc de Blancs. I'm told it has creamy bubble finesse with almond-orange notes."

"Sounds delicious."

He returned her smile as he filled a tulip shaped flute. "Might I have a word with you in private?"

Before she could take a sip, he steered her into an adjoining room. Two rows of cushy leather seats faced a large flat-screen monitor. Elle braced herself against the back of one of chairs.

Lord Severn studied her, nostrils flared, inhaling the air between them. "Quite extraordinary, your scent."

She took a gulp of champagne before answering. "I'm sorry, was that a compliment?"

"'The flowers of oak, blossoms of broom and of meadowsweet...'" The man waxed poetic as liquid mercury eyes moved over her. "'...from those they conjured the fairest and most beautiful maiden anyone had ever seen.'"

His own wistful smile seemed to break the spell. "An ancient tale from our origins. And a compliment to be sure. Have you heard of the Eve Gene?"

Elle shook her head.

"You are a carrier of the gene from whom all living wolfen descend in an unbroken line, through your own mother—and all the mothers of those mothers—until the lineage converges on a single female. She is called Eve for lack of a better name."

"You say I'm *a* carrier—not *the* carrier—so there must be others."

"Many are lost to us." His direct gaze faltered a bit. "But perhaps not for long."

She managed a nod. Things were starting to fall into place. So much so, she felt a pout coming on. "Is this the reason why I'm being chased by wolfen?"

"You are pure blooded, my dear. A rarified female and difficult to detect when on the lycanthrope suppressant."

Elle didn't bother to hide her thoughts. "First, the supply of *lycosopene* is cut off. Then, as its protection weakens…" A chill ran down her spine. She'd always known the risks that came with exposure, perhaps she just never fully believed it.

His thin smile offered small comfort. "I'm afraid you are all in great demand…and grave danger. Gene pools have been weakened over the past century. Many of the packs are looking to improve their line, in particular, their powers."

"Powers…" Elle murmured. She'd seen Abelseth do things that made a hash out of physical universe, from Newton's laws of motion to quantum mechanics. Extraordinary acts she never knew wolfen were capable of. Even more troubling, strange things were starting to happen around her, events she had little or no control over.

She backed away. "Why are you telling me all this?"

Dark pupils haloed by silver followed her retreat. "My dear, I should think it obvious."

His lordship terrified Elle with his talk of the Eve Gene and rarified females. As if she, and others like her, were prize brood mares.

Lord Severn cut her off near the door. "One last thing." He held up a finger. "We will need to continue to produce small quantities of lycanthrope suppressant. It is my intention to protect our…" He hesitated, before finishing his thought. "…young females such as yourself." His tight-lipped smile less reassuring than ever. "Might you by any chance have an address for Ignatius Binns? Any sort of contact information would help."

"Iggy was just the distributor—I doubt—" Elle stopped herself.

She needed to be careful what she revealed about the chemist, though in point of fact, no one knew much about him. It was he who had developed the formulation and the time-release capsules, which at this juncture, might very well be lost forever.

What made the unknown scientist truly remarkable was his ability to synthesize the *Aconitum* poison at the nano-molecular level. Enough to deaden her wolf nature, and render her scent completely untraceable, but otherwise leave a person healthy and human.

She met Lord Severn's prying gaze directly. Perhaps she would impart a morsel of information and hope it would suffice. "Iggy would call the last Monday of every month—the number was always different."

"Yes, of course he'd use burners." Lord Severn mused aloud.

Elle remembered something else. "Just before the large black wolf appeared in the station, I received a text—running late." She dug her phone out of her purse and found the number. "Here it is." She held up the screen. "It's possible the phone hasn't been destroyed yet."

Lord Severn opened the door and called in one of Maccon's men, who copied down the number.

She used the momentary intrusion as an excuse to part ways. "Well, I'm off to find Abby." She bobbed her head. "Your lordship."

Elle zigged then zagged her way through the crowded room, keeping an eye on Lord Severn. She hadn't a clue how this man knew about Iggy or the lycosopene. At this point, all she wanted to do was find Abelseth. He was the only one she trusted and she desperately needed answers.

C h a p t e r

NINE

Abelseth vs. Ex Cereberus

"Elle is frightened, as are many females like her," Abelseth explained behind closed doors. "They've been brought up to believe we're all beasts."

"Partially true." Maccon grinned.

He stared across the table at his brother. "These past two nights have no doubt confirmed it for her."

"How long has she been off the suppressant?" Phelan sat at his brother's right side. His posh cousin was obviously an important member of Maccon's counsel. "Have to ask, her pheromones are off the—"

The flash of warning in his eyes sent Phelan deeper into his leather chair. "No more than seventy-two hours—give or take. Which accounts for the abduction attempt last night. They tried again this evening."

"I say better us than them. Blooded females are scarce. Mate her, Abby," Maccon growled, "because if you don't, I will."

His glare drilled into his sibling. "You are already mated."

Maccon shrugged. "These are hard times, exceptions can and will be made."

Abelseth struggled to hold fierce emotions inside his body. His physical attraction to Elle could hardly be in doubt. He'd made it clear to every male at the party that this rare female was his. And yet his brother and assorted advisors were ready to pounce—steal the girl out from under his nose.

"She's just off the suppressant and wants nothing to do with our kind," he answered, his tone measured, icy.

Maccon emptied his glass. "Change her mind."

Phelan's lip curled. "She certainly appears to want you."

"You don't—none of you know this young woman."

Macon laced his fingers together and sat back. "Tell us about her."

He took his time answering. "She's intuitive, as well as intelligent—"

"And beautiful," his brother interrupted, "an irresistible combination."

"She can also be difficult, challenging…" Tired of trading withering looks with his brother, he was purposely evasive. But he'd be damned if he'd give up much about her. "Of course I wouldn't have it any other way."

"Are you in love, Abby?" His brother's insolent grin rankled.

This was not going brilliantly. He rose from his chair. "This time, you won't get the girl, little brother." He kicked the chair back and strode across the room.

"You're not leaving, are you?" Maccon called

after him. "The night is young…Abby?"

"Stay away from her." He slammed the door and ran straight into the pack leader's pale-faced mate.

Abelseth drew back. "Well, this is awkward. You didn't—Izzy—did you hear any of that nonsense?"

She grabbed his hand and led him out a sliding glass door to an expansive multi-tiered terrace. The garden overlooked the Thames with a spectacular view of London.

From the upper level, Abelseth watched her stroll along the balcony railing. "What's going on between you and Maccon?"

"Besides his infidelities?" She shrugged. "My life is hunky-dory." She reached behind her dress and unzipped. The dress fell around her feet.

"Izzy, why are you doing this?"

"You heard why." She stepped out of the dress, pivoting toward him. Small perfect breasts, beautiful as always. A tiny triangle of lace narrowed into thin strings that arched over her hips. "It will hurt him—at very least bruise his ego. And I'll make sure he finds out."

The wicked little temptress was tempting, all right. "Five years is a long time, Izzy." He might never completely forgive Maccon for stealing her away, but his rage over the betrayal had vanished. And then there was Izzy herself.

He descended a few shallow steps. "You didn't have to go with him, did you?"

"I've missed you, Abby." She ran her hands up her body and plucked at her nipples.

He sensed eyes on his back, coming from the wall

of glass behind them. A side of his mouth twitched. "Have your friends seen enough, or shall I pretend to make a move—give them something to gasp over?"

Her eyes darted to something or someone behind him.

He turned in time to see Elle slip between party gawkers and dash away.

Izzy called after him as he vanished into the drift. "He wants your girl, Abby, don't let her out of your sight this time."

Abelseth leaned against the Mini Cooper and waited for her to exit the tower. *Wherever you're headed, Elle, I'm going with you.*

Message sent.

The long-legged beauty stepped out of the building and approached him warily. "And how exactly do I explain you to my mother?"

"I can be your friend or lover—you decide."

She dug in her purse for her keys. "Tell me, Abby, does it have to be either-or? Are you capable of being a friend and a lover?"

His lips twitched. "Is this a test?"

"What was that striptease all about on the terrace?" She folded her arms under her chest and waited.

"Not a pretty story. But if you insist—"

"Do not lie to me, Abelseth. They were quite pretty. And yes, I insist."

He rather liked her stubborn, territorial nature— and she was a fighter. "Izzy overheard Maccon threaten to mate you if I didn't. Apparently, there have been other infidelities. The scene on the terrace was designed by her to bruise his ego. I didn't touch her—"

"I know," she noted quietly. The ends of her mouth tilted up. Not a bad sign after what he'd just revealed to her.

"We need time to talk, Elle. We both want information, explanations…assurances." He could only hope that she was curious enough about her wolf nature that she'd push past her fears. "And hers are not half as pretty as yours."

A lovely swath of pink colored her cheeks as she unlocked the car. "Bradford-on-Avon is two hours away. Plenty of time to decide how to introduce you to mummy."

His nose itched, which nearly always meant a disturbance in the drift. They had perhaps seconds before the pack arrived. He opened the door and shoved her inside the car.

Down the block, a half dozen wolfen assembled on the sidewalk. More formidable this time, all of them large and muscled. He recognized several faces from the meeting room in the Underground.

"Get out of here—quickly, Elle!"

*

Elle willed her hand to stop shaking. "Damn you, get in there." The key finally slipped into the ignition, and she stomped on the accelerator.

The Mini roared out of the parking space.

Halfway down the lane, she caught a glimpse of Abelseth in the rearview mirror. The pack had surrounded him. Or was he drawing them in, inviting confrontation?

She moved her foot to the brake pedal, but something held her back.

Faster, love—do not stop until you're well out of town.

An hour later, she relaxed her white-knuckle grip on the steering wheel. Holy crikey, mother of all mothers, there really was a rabbit hole! And a violent one at that.

As a girl, she'd been told spine-chilling tales about the wolfen underworld. But this—this was as dangerous as it was mysterious. And she'd left London with a heavy heart.

Abelseth's abilities went beyond the extraordinary. In fact, they were akin to magic. Not the Harry Potter *wingardium leviosa* sort of spell—more like the power of Thor, only he wasn't a superhero. Or was he?

She'd caught a glimpse of the carnage as she sped away from the tower. Healthy bodies tossed into energetic space, the horrifying sight of bones and flesh being separated into tiny particles of matter and "disappeared" into the strange otherworld called the drift.

On the outskirts of town, a large black creature— half man, half wolf—had landed in the road ahead and she'd blown through him without the slightest hesitation. Abelseth had taught her that. In fact, he'd given her the tools she needed to survive an onslaught of abductors as long as she drove like a woman possessed.

Excited by the chase, and lack of suppressant, particles of wolf matter bubbled quietly in her veins. A wild thing simmered just below the surface. And the urges were so intoxicating. Elle sucked in a breath and exhaled slowly. It was only a matter of time before she experienced a shift, either accidental or on purpose.

She turned off the M4 for petrol.

Nightmarish images continued to cyclone in her head.

From the moment she'd pulled away from the curb, Mini tires squealing, she'd missed everything about him. His delicious spicy scent, his reassuring voice, and those beautiful crystalline eyes. Honest eyes, whether they were searching her soul or mentally undressing her.

She exhaled a sigh. Mostly, she missed his stoic, steadfast presence.

On the motorway tonight, she'd searched for him in every passing car, squinted past glaring headlights, scrutinized shadows on the side of the road. She turned into the Esso Express, feeling sulky and out of sorts.

Her heart skipped a beat.

A tall, imposing man wearing a long coat pivoted as she drove the car under the station canopy. Abelseth stood between petrol pumps looking a bit worse for wear.

Elle climbed out of the car.

"Where are we?" he croaked, huskily.

"Just outside Swindon." She closed the door and moved closer. "What, no GPS locator in the drift?"

217

His one-sided grin made him flinch. He was in pain. A crescent shaped cut slashed through his left eyebrow. His upper lip was split, and there was a good-sized bruise on his right cheek. "You're looking a bit trampled." She moved her hands up the lapels of his coat.

"I would have caught up sooner, but I ran into a few more Exers along the way."

"And they ran into you." She kissed him gently on the mouth. "Don't scare me like that," she whispered. "I thought I'd lost you." He tasted of blood and salty sweat, and before she could control herself, she licked the split on his lip.

Then she licked again.

Elle waited for the dark red slice to close seamlessly and fade. "Wolf saliva contains healing properties."

His gaze never left her. "So I've heard."

Standing on tip-toe, she healed the cut over his eye, and the scrape across the bridge of his nose. Midway through her descent, he caught and kissed her softly, pulling her so close he gasped.

"Bruised ribs?" she asked, palpitating gently.

"Nothing a shift won't fix." He kissed her again, harder this time, opening her lips with his tongue, and sending a shot of electricity through her body.

She came up for air light-headed, with her heart racing. Overwhelmed by emotion, she leaned into him. "I feel as though I'm dissembling underwater, drowning in you."

He tilted her chin up. "As am I."

She inhaled the warmth of his breath. "Why is

that?"

"Perhaps we're fighting this thing—you and I—too much."

His insight was perhaps a bit too insightful. Caught off guard, she backed away. "You pump, while I'll scare up a few supplies."

Elle purchased two bottles of water, an Aero chocolate bar and a package of baby wipes. While she cleaned his cuts and scrapes, he put away a few chocolate squares.

He held out a piece. "Open."

The light chocolate treat melted in her mouth. "M-mm, who knew air and chocolate could taste so good?" She examined his face. "Better. Now let's see about the rest of you." She unbuttoned his shirt. "I know, cheeky of me."

The sweep of another vehicle's headlamps briefly illuminated the red blotches that spread across his torso. Shadows and light played over his chest and abs. He had the body of a footballer, lean and not too bulky, with a light mat of chest hair that narrowed and disappeared beneath his belt.

Elle dipped lower and nuzzled fur. Ab muscles shivered under her tongue as she licked the taut flesh. She inhaled his scent—spicy, like hot rum, but also musky with subtle notes of cedar or sandalwood.

"In my condition, arousal can be…" He pushed away. "I could shift with little control."

She sat back in the driver's seat and stared. He was aroused. And his admission gave her naughty, tantalizing thoughts about his wilder side. "Which is better—sex as a wolf or a human?"

He seemed a bit taken back. "Generally, we copulate as humans. Wolf sex leaves one vulnerable to attack. It can be—" He paused, searching for words. "A male wolf gets 'locked' inside the female for up to half an hour."

Locked inside her. She found it hard to take her eyes off the battered warrior, more sublimely handsome than she'd ever seen him.

For half an hour. She tried picturing him as a wolf with those deadly piercing blue eyes—his body covered in thick fur...rubbing...nuzzling her.

"Elle?" He smiled a knowing smile.

She snapped out of her bestial reverie, cheeks burning. He'd read her secret thoughts.

Stay out of my head!

He laughed out loud. It was the first unguarded moment of elation she'd ever heard from Abelseth and it was so completely spontaneous and joyful, she smiled. "So sex as a wolf is out of the question."

"Not...completely out of the question." He did a cute sort of double-take, as if he could not quite believe they were having a casual chat about wolf sex. He dipped his head to peer out the rear window. "And there's nothing I'd enjoy more than to enlighten you further, but my first priority is to get you safely to Bradford-on-Avon." He buttoned his shirt. "I can take the wheel if you like."

Duty first.

There were times, like now, when the man's grace and nobility adorned him like a halo. A wolf prince who never had to remind himself to man-up.

"You've done enough for now." She turned the

key and the engine rumbled to life. "For the next hour or so, I'd like to have a good long chat about what's going on." She turned onto the motorway and accelerated.

"Keep our speed over ninety," he advised. "It makes the chase difficult and a landing nearly impossible." She whipped a glance his way, and he grinned. "I'm a copper, I can fix a speeding ticket."

Elle stepped on it. "We haven't lost them yet?"

"Sooner or later a scout will pick up our scent." He checked his side mirror. She had to admit, she took comfort in having him along for the ride.

"I understand it's hard for you to trust, Elle, particularly after last night and this evening, but in order to help you, I need to know something of your history. Perhaps you could start with your wolf clan?"

Detective Inspector Durant had resurfaced, and he was determined to hear her story. Elle sucked in air and thought about how and where she might begin.

"You need to understand something. Mother and I belong to no pack, and have little to do with the Wyvern clan. We maintain few contacts and rely on no one…" Elle hesitated. "At least…that is what I used to believe."

She thought about her coworkers at Chelsea Gardens. Recently, she had come to suspect that several of them were wolfen. Friendlies to be sure, but the idea was as shocking as it was comforting. As if unseen fairy godparents had been assigned to watch over her.

"When I was still in primaries, my father died suddenly. The coroner called it an accidental poisoning." Her grip tightened on the steering wheel. "They made his death sound like an unlucky mishap. Mother and I didn't quite believe that. Can you imagine a horticulturist of my father's experience mistaking wolfsbane for delphinium? Not likely," she huffed.

"No one took you in?"

"One of the local packs offered," she continued, "but mother wouldn't hear of it. After the funeral, they pleaded with her—"

"They?" he interrupted. "Try to be specific, it will help."

"Clan higher-ups came calling, distinguished looking gentlemen. Mother told me to stay in my room and latch the door—not to come out until she gave the all clear." Elle sneaked a glance at the male wolf beside her. "I remember my knees knocking, even as I pressed my ear to the door, ready to fight them off."

"Not surprising. You're quite brave, Elle."

She slanted a skeptical glance at him. "After they left, Mother and I packed in the middle of the night. Two people came and drove us to a tower beside the river."

"The Avon?"

She nodded. "A rather queer house, four or five stories high, with a mansard roof. We stayed there for several days before they relocated us." She increased speed, passing slower cars on the motorway. "Eventually, we were settled into our own residence. I remember being fearful at first. We kept to ourselves, mostly. As time went on, we made

Bradford-on-Avon our home."

Eyes ever on the alert, he remained silent for a moment. "I take it you had a private chat with my uncle this evening."

Elle quickly recapped her encounter with Lord Severn. "He has a strange way about him. A bit of a creeper, wouldn't you say?" She caught the bare semblance of a smile.

"Uncle Algernon is a crafty sort, and you're wise not to trust him. But in your case, I believe he means well. I suspect he's trying to get ahead of a predatory situation that could escalate rapidly."

She thought about the other females like her. As the supply of suppressant dried up, they would all be hunted down and abducted. "He who controls the formula controls all the females on the suppressant."

"Would you have it be Ex Cerberus or the Lords?"

His words, though spoken softly, spiked the hairs on the back of her neck. "And why should males of either pack be put in charge of the suppressant?" She chewed her bottom lip. "For God's sake, is your uncle aware we're living in the third millennium, A.D.? All this talk of mating blooded females. It's worse than medieval. We're not druid virgins to be captured and bred to the high priests. I have a life, a career that I'm passionate about—can this really be happening in the twenty-first century?"

Elle paused for a breath. She needed to get a grip, and their exit ramp was coming up. She turned off the motorway, and stole a quick glance at his furrowed brow.

"We very likely crawled out of the same chalky

soil as the druids. Even so, we've made progress." The irony in his voice turned sober. "A female occupies the highest seat of power in my clan."

She did a quick double-take. "And you are?"

"Pendragon."

Elle wrinkled her nose. "Royal wolfen. I might have guessed."

"We split from Wyvern centuries ago—a clan known for its ferocious, dragon-like females." She caught the upturn at the ends his mouth. "I assume you are aware there's been a rapprochement. Our clans have realigned."

"How can you call it progress when young women will be forced into marriage—bare children to males not of their choosing? Do they plan on shuttering us away? How could they possibly keep this a secret?"

The moment she uttered the words she realized the folly of her statement. Wolfen had kept all of it a secret—the clans, the packs, the power they wielded—for ages. Why would it be any different now?

"Elle, we're not going to let that happen." Something in the tenor of his voice, deadly calm and unwavering, eased her anxiety.

The road narrowed as it wound its way through farmland and quaint villages. Though little could be seen in the dark, the gently rolling hills and valleys of Wiltshire bore the marks of their ancient culture. The neolithic stone circle at Avebury, the stately monoliths of Stonehenge on the Salisbury plain. Never mind the enigma that was Silbury Hill, and those luminous orbs that hovered over the crop circles…

Our little corner of England has been down the rabbit hole for eons. Abelseth had impressive supernatural abilities, telepathy being one of them. More than once he'd spoken to her in her mind, as well as snooped about in her thoughts.

She stopped the car at a rail crossing. "Our little corner?"

"I was brought up not far from here. Northeast of Chippenham, in Castle Combe."

He constantly astounded her. Once again, she stared at him. "My mum was born in Castle Combe."

Things had become uncomfortably cozy between them, and now it appeared they shared kin. "Since we are both blooded lycanthrope," her words rushed out in a weak, breathy whisper. "Good God, we're probably related."

"Third or fourth cousins twice removed… hopefully." His half-smile made her cheeks burn. "The train has passed, you can go now."

Elle stomped on the accelerator pedal. All this talk of blooded females and mating was making her horny and irritable. She put the Mini through its paces and didn't slow down until they reached the outskirts of Bradford-on-Avon.

"After we resettled, Mother took a job working as a maid at Wolley Grange." She pointed to the luxury hotel which had once been a grand manor house. The grounds were hard to see in the dark, but its windows blazed with light. "She's the day manager nowadays. Growing up, I remember it was always important to keep a low profile. As time went on, we made friends and have lived here quite happily."

"Then you went off to school."

Elle pulled up to a charming village townhouse, parking alongside a low stone wall. "Mother was anxious, understandably, what with my affliction."

He flinched, and Elle bit her tongue. "That was a bit harsh, sorry." A rush of heat warmed her cheeks. "It's just that I don't know the wolf in me. I'm afraid of her. She's like…a dark passenger."

His eyes glistened in the dim light, liquid and vulnerable. As expansive and thrilling as a clear sky on a windy day, and yet filled with the wisdom of the ages. Eyes that understood honor and gallantry, and how to keep powerful secrets. Elle couldn't help trembling under his gaze. Perhaps the shiver had more to do with the way he studied her, measured, with strong hints of empathy and desire.

"Come here." He pulled her close and swept a few loose waves off her face. "You survived, Elle— better than survived, you flourished. But you are in transition during a dangerous time. Trust me enough to let me help you."

In just a few hours this evening, Abelseth had gone from a handsome, eccentric acquaintance, to a colossally important companion in arms. Between soft kisses, she managed a few coherent thoughts. "I'm beginning to see that in some ways, even though she meant well, Mother has kept too many secrets."

He nuzzled her nose. "It would seem so."

C h a p t e r

TEN

Elle discovers that love is thicker than blood.

Abelseth joined Elle on the porch steps. "You realize you're taking me home to meet your mother."

"I am not!" she protested, her laughter joining his. She rolled her eyes and knocked. "I suppose, technically, I am."

"Don't be too hard on her. She believes she's protecting you."

"The entire house is slipcovered in chintz," she whispered. "There, you've been warned." Her second rap on the door was louder.

The door creaked open on its own, revealing a dark entry and darker hallway.

Elle turned to him. "Not good."

Abelseth leaned out over the porch and checked a window. "A single light on in the parlor. Was she expecting you?"

"We texted late this afternoon." Elle's nose twitched. "What is that?" She inhaled another whiff.

Abelseth sniffed the air. "Something familiar about the scent."

Elle poked her head in the door. "Mummy?"

Do not go in there, Elle! Abelseth had never used

his command head voice with her and she jumped back. "Let me go first," he whispered.

He stepped over the threshold and waited. Nothing—then a thumping sound and some thrashing about.

"Someone's in the cellar," Elle whispered. "Down the hallway to the right."

Abelseth moved silently toward a narrow door.

More thumping and stair climbing. The knob turned and shook so violently, he thought it might come unhinged. The door burst open and an attractive, middle-aged woman stood in hallway.

She stared at him. "What are you doing in my house?" The color noticeably drained from her face, still, the woman kept her wits about her.

"D.I. Durant, New Scotland Yard, you must be Mrs. Hathaway." Ash blonde hair, cut in a shoulder-length bob framed an attractive face, with lovely gray-green eyes that lit up at the sight of her daughter.

"Elle, darling!" She moved past him to give her a hug.

"Hello, Mummy."

"You didn't mention you were bringing a friend." Her mother's gaze shifted to him, curious with a bit of trepidation, perhaps? "What a lovely surprise."

"Abelseth Durant, I'd like you to meet my mother, Violet Hathaway."

He nodded his head. "Mrs. Hathaway. Apologies for the rude entrance—it's just that we found this open." He shut the door behind Elle.

"You are with the police, Mr. Durant?" her mother queried weakly.

"Homicide Task Force, CID," he clarified. "Don't be alarmed, this isn't an official call. And please, call me Abelseth."

"Only if you call me Violet." One didn't have to be clairvoyant to read the concern in her eyes. "You work for the Metropolitan Police, yet I suspect there is more to you than meets the eye." Her mother ushered them into the parlor. "Unusual given name. In fact, I haven't heard the name Abelseth since Elle was in primary school."

He met her mother's gaze directly. "Yes, I believe we both hail from—"

"Castle Combe." Violet reached up and gently traced the cut over his eye.

If there was such a thing as a wolfen mind meld this was it. Elle's mother would confirm what she'd already guessed, that he was wolfen. In fact, he suspected she knew more about him than her own daughter did.

Softer eyes studied him. "A shift would do you good, mend those cuts and bruises."

He nodded. "I'm afraid Elle is in rather grave danger. We've spent the past two days dodging a pack of rogue wolves. Last night, there was a failed abduction. She needs to learn our ways quickly."

"Abby is my friend and bodyguard." Elle blurted out. "He didn't apply for the job, it has been sort of…thrust upon him." She moved further inside the parlor and turned on a lamp. "Pottering about in the dark, what's got into you, Mummy?"

"The same pack made another attempt this evening," he added.

Violet's brows squiggled a bit. "I've had a few unusual encounters myself of late. Can't say I wasn't expecting something like this." Cool as a cucumber, she studied both their faces. "Cup'a tea, dears?"

A sharp rap at the door startled everyone.

"Exers wouldn't bother to knock." He ventured down the hallway. "Remain here and stay quiet." The two women hid at the top of the cellar steps.

He opened the front door and blinked. "Mother?"

"Abelseth, you look awful, fighting again? Who was it this time?"

"Ex Cereberus."

"Those horrid thugs?" His mother swept into the foyer and kissed him on both cheeks. "You need a good shift."

"Yes, it's been suggested." Mildly amused, as well as curious, he followed her fluttering cape into the parlor. "Might I ask what brings you to Bradford-on-Avon?"

"An urgent text from your Uncle Algernon." A force of nature, Tallis Bodicca Durant rarely missed a trick. Her keen gaze swept the dark corners of the room. "Vi—is that you?"

Mother and daughter emerged from behind the cellar door. Violet crept closer, eyes wide. "Tallis, how long has it been?"

The two women hugged, fussed over each other, then embraced again. He caught Elle's eye, and she returned an equally quizzical look. It would seem their mothers were old chums.

Two male guards stationed themselves inside the door, while two more manned the porch steps.

Abelseth gave the men a good once over. "I see you've arrived with an entourage."

"I'm afraid there is no time to chat, perhaps we can catch up on the road?" His mother returned to Violet. "We must leave for the safe house—pack a few things—quickly, Vi."

"I can't believe this is happening again," Violet's brow furrowed, worry evident on her face.

"Ghastly," his mother agreed. "There is no more suppressant in London and the supply is scarce everywhere else. Elle needs our protection."

Violet disappeared up a staircase, her lips set in a grim line.

His mother signaled one of the guards. "Derek, go with her."

Elle sidled closer to him. "I believe your mother may have helped us disappear years ago," she whispered.

"And you must be Luella." His mother took in every detail. "Oh, my dear, you are lovely." She continued to study Elle. "You may not remember it, but you and my son met years ago."

Elle shook her head. "I'm sorry—"

One of the outside men interrupted. "We'll need the keys to her car."

"Do you wish to pack a few things, dear?" his mother asked.

Elle handed over her keys. "My overnight bag is in the Mini."

In no time the house was shuttered and they were loaded into cars. Abelseth sandwiched himself between the Hathaway women in the back of the

Bentley, with his mother, a driver and a bodyguard in front. The remaining two men followed in Elle's car.

As they roared off into the night, his mother angled in her seat, taking the three of them in. "Oh, Vi, you do realize they found each other, despite our interference?"

Abelseth arched a brow. "What sort of interference?"

"My dear beautiful boy." His mother smiled. "You two were promised to each other the moment Elle was born."

*

Abelseth sat on the edge of the terrace and Elle took the next step down, tucking herself between his legs. High above, framed by a black velvet sky, Weir House loomed over them. What the country house lacked in comfort, it made up for in fortress-like amenities.

Built on a bend of the River Avon, the stronghold included the towering manse, and several outbuildings protected by a walled courtyard, and a small private army. Beyond the iron gate, a narrow road meandered past a strip of forest that ran along the river. On the west side of the road, grain fields surrounded the compound.

Safe enough for now.

Abelseth listened to the pleasant tinkle of female laughter drifitng down from a window high above.

"Tallis and Violet are having a good chin-wag," he commented softly.

Elle leaned back into his chest. "Sounds like they're just getting started. This could go on for hours."

He rubbed his beard scruff against the fine hairs at her temple. "Sorry about Mother."

"Your mother? What about mine?" Elle shook her head in disbelief. "Violet's gone barmy."

He snorted a soft laugh. "How does it feel, knowing we were promised to each other years ago?"

"Completely unreal." She sighed. "Like we're characters in a fairy tale."

Abelseth did a quick mental replay of the evening, in particular, their journey to the Pendragon stronghold. The getaway car had been driven at a blistering pace, and upon arrival at Weir House, they'd settled in quickly, meeting for a nightcap in the drawing room.

After several toasts, and a loosening of inhibitions, both mothers had decided that he and Elle should pair up immediately. A slightly tipsy way of saying, sorry to keep you two apart all these years, but let's formalize the marriage in a civil ceremony as soon as possible.

Implied in their decision was that Abelseth would mate Elle—as in copulate with her. And it must be done immediately. A rosy-red blush had swept across Elle's cheeks, which immediately prompted wicked thoughts on his part. Most of them having to do with Elle stark naked, riding his erect phallus, waves of unruly hair tossed over her shoulders as he plunged in deep.

He'd slammed a shot of whiskey down his throat

to get the images out his head. "I'm curious about this mating arrangement between our clans." His gaze moved between the two meddling co-conspirators.

Mother had avoided his scrutiny by refilling their glasses. "This is a fine burgundy, care for some?" She held up the bottle.

"I'll stick with the single malt," he bit out.

Out of fear or protection, his mother was being evasive. She picked up a decanter and poured him another whiskey.

This time he asked in a softer voice. "Please enlighten me, Mother."

She exhaled a sigh. "Depending on scarcity, there have always been abductions of pure blooded females."

He nodded. "The abominable practice goes back centuries."

"Yes, well..." His mother sidled off, furtively. "Not long after Elle's father was murdered, the abductions started again. For a time, we trusted no one, so we hid her away."

Abelseth found her explanation strained, and still somewhat evasive. "Bring us up to date, if you would."

"As you know, the great unrest escalated—the clan wars came and went—new alliances were made, old ones mended..."

"The Pendragon and Wyvern clans realigned," he added. His gaze followed her as she paced the room.

"Not long after the war, your father died. Then you and Maccon had your falling out, and you stepped down from the Lords." Her shrug had seemed honest enough, and it was hard to miss the sparkle in her eyes. "There didn't seem to be much point in pairing the two of you...until now."

Abelseth felt a tug at his sleeve.

"Hey—" Elle pulled him out of his thoughts and back to her. "How do you feel about all this talk about us?"

"As much as I'd like to tell them both to—" She placed a finger over his mouth which he removed. "I was about to say our mothers' scheme, however startling, may be the only way to keep you safe. And there is also the matter of your wolf. You need to learn basic skills—shifting, drifting—then all the arts. The Exers will move on eventually, Uncle will see to it. In the meantime, I can run them off."

She leaned into his chest. "Is it hard to be both human and wolfen? I've been told there are strong urges."

"The physical part takes practice, a bit of discipline. Exercise helps. I try to shift at least once a week, go for a good long four-legged run in Hamstead Heath Woods."

Her eyes grew wide, and her pupils dilated. "Will you bite me?"

"Made wolves are bitten. All you require is a quickening." When her eyebrows did that squiggly thing, he clarified. "I've already begun to awaken you."

"Our dance in the drift?"

He nodded. "That and..." He slipped his hand under her sweater. "Getting physical with you." Splayed fingers moved over ribs barely felt, to the sheer fabric of her bra. Her nipple hardened under the brush of his thumb, and she moaned softly.

She reached up and pulled him close, delivering soft kisses and sensuous bites. The faintest, playful nip aroused him, more than any female he'd ever known. He needed to mate with her, but would not do so quickly or use force. Elle was wary, skittish, and at the moment, his number one task was to guide her through her first shift and make sure she returned to human form.

"Is it painful?" she asked.

"A shift is never painless, but there are things I can do to help."

"Like?" Starlight glistened in her eyes. There had always been a lovely vulnerability about Elle, yet she was also strong and brave, as she would have to be when the change came.

He nuzzled her ear. "Go up to your room and remove all your clothes. Wear something easy to get in and out of—a slip or nightgown, and wait for my signal."

She caught her breath. "We're doing this tonight?"

Chapter

ELEVEN

Elle finds her wild. And her heart.

A handful of pebbles scattered across the window pane. Elle peered through the glass to the courtyard below. A statuesque figure stood far below, waiting for her.

He appeared cool, even dispassionate at times, but she had come to understand something about his stoic, inner strength as well as his more public personae, that of the dashing, handsome police detective. It would seem Abelseth Durant was in complete control of himself…until he wasn't.

Having never experienced his wolf, she could only sense the wildness in his nature. But there were strong hints about his unknown side. His strength of heart, his fierce gaze, and the primal magnetism he used to rally the forces of a mysterious universe to do his bidding.

Elle shivered.

Worst of all—no, best of all, she'd gotten a taste of his hidden passions. His savage kisses, the caress of his hands on her body, and how those skilled fingers of his knew exactly how to arouse the wanton she-wolf.

The side of her that was winning.

At odds with her feelings, she paced a circle around her small room. So why did she feel so conflicted? For one thing, she hardly knew him. And for all his strengths, there were equally frightening aspects to his character. She'd seen him dispose of his enemies in ways that were horrifying. Bodies bounced off walls, bones ground to a pulp, or shredded into pink mist and tossed into the drift.

There was also the question of honesty. But since all wolfen were born into a cult of secrecy and lies, it was hardly something she could call him on. Piled on top of that was his legacy.

There was no question he was a man of destiny, whether he liked it or not. His pack knew it, and most certainly his family did. Now, he was being forced into the role of progenitor. Alpha mate to a female of little consequence, but that she was pure-blooded lycanthrope.

Elle bristled at the thought. He would mate and marry her, not out of love, but of duty. And perhaps there was another cause, as well. He wished to protect her from rival packs who would have little regard for her happiness.

But what if...the sudden thought so disturbed, her heart pounded in her chest. What if this muddled nightmare she found herself in was just another abduction? What if this rescue in the middle of the night, was a clever Pendragon ruse?

Elle took slow deep breaths to calm herself. She needed to keep a clear head so she could formulate a getaway plan. Opening her overnight bag, she changed into her favorite nightshift, soft and nearly transparent from years of laundering. She moved to the vanity table and unpinned her hair.

The window lock squeaked, and an icy chill tingled down her spine. Elle looked up into the mirror as Abelseth's reflection appeared. She set down her hair brush and turned around. He perched on the roof just outside glass panes. The handsomest gargoyle in the history of gargoyles.

The window sash lifted on its own. He opened his coat and she was instantly swept into his arms. He buttoned the coat around her as they spun through the air. Starlight swirled around his head, as they skimmed the surface of the drift and landed in the strip of woods that ran along the riverbank.

Elle shivered and the wolf quiver felt natural, head to tail.

"Cold?"

She shook her head. "It's more of a tingly feeling, like start of an itch."

"As if you're in the wrong skin." He stroked her back in that comforting way of his.

Her nostrils flared, picking up on his earthy, woodsy scent, and even more intoxicating, his wolf essence.

"I can feel her stirring," he whispered. He released her and pivoted away, walking deeper into the stand of trees. The forest that enveloped him turned luminous and inviting, as if he was painting the way with fairy light.

The very idea of escape suddenly felt wrong and foolish. Elle followed after, crushing leaves and stepping on twigs. This was not the time to cut and run. Anyway, she'd just be caught and forced to surrender.

Her bare feet should be tender but they weren't. The chill in the air felt soothing, even sensuous. And that itchy sensation had crystallized into a slow, seductive burn.

Up ahead, Abelseth waited for her. His beautiful eyes gleamed with the promise of something feral and passionate between them.

Her belly quivered as she entered the small clearing. They were standing on top of an expansive mound of springy turf. The moss-like grass felt smooth and cool underfoot. "You're staring at me."

He nodded. "At Elle, wearing next to nothing. Moonlight illuminating every beautiful curve."

He moved closer.

She shied away.

He stepped forward.

She stepped back.

His gaze narrowed. "Are you afraid of me?"

"No."

"Angry?"

"No!" She cringed a little, knowing full well she didn't look happy. "Yes." She shook her head. "I don't know—I'm confused—what if I don't want to be mated?" She wrung her hands. "Try not to take this personally…"

"What's bothering you, Elle?" His gaze was fierce, but his voice remained gentle. Enough to give her the courage to confront him. Watch his reaction.

With her trust in him dangling by a thread, she exhaled the words. "What if I'm being abducted by the Lords right now? What if this has all been carefully orchestrated to make it look like a rescue when—"

He cut her off. "When in fact, they're mating and marrying you off to Abelseth Durant." He released a harsh sigh. "Or course it's possible, but it doesn't matter anymore."

Her eyebrows squiggled up and down. "Why doesn't it matter?"

"Elle, I'm ready to mate you, marry you, because I want to, not because of some conspiracy. I give you my word, I play no role in any such plot."

She eyeballed him warily and he returned a hard-edged stare.

Finally, he blinked. "Can I assure you that my mother—our mothers—for that matter, aren't unwitting players in a larger scheme orchestrated by my uncle? I cannot."

Utterly horrified and yet giddy with hope, she bit back a smile. "So, you've had similar thoughts."

"The night you were abducted I find my posh cousin among the Exers. Not exactly how Phelan rolls. The next morning, Uncle tracks me down in London for a chat about police work. He also happens to mention a certain witness to the crime." He shook his head. "And Maccon's threat tonight, a bit over the top, wouldn't you say?"

She inched closer. "How long have you known?"

"I don't believe we know anything for certain... yet."

She reached up, tracing the cut above his eyebrow with her finger. "Rather a cruel bit of matchmaking."

"I suppose they had to make it look good." His mouth tilted upward.

The fierce wild thing thrashed around inside her, whispering naughty thoughts. "I want you inside me." She blurted the words out, along with a pink tongue, which she swept under the curve of his upper lip.

He searched her face. "Am I speaking with Elle or her wolf?"

"Shameless, isn't she?" Her cheeks flamed with heat as she pressed closer. "We need a plan of our own," she whispered. "And then you will mate me."

His gaze dropped to her mouth. "Happy to oblige…both of you."

"This pull between us is real, and goes far beyond our mothers' meddling." Elle ripped open his shirt, raking her fingernails over his chest.

He sucked air through his teeth. "Our best course of action is to do nothing."

"Nothing?" she murmured.

"We play along, gather evidence," he gasped as her lips brushed over his neck and chest. "And when the time is right, we play our cards."

Had the creature inside her just removed his shirt? Did it matter? All Elle could think about was his hands on her body, exploring. "Some ferocious sex and no more talk would be lovely right about now." Her breath buffeted off his skin, as she licked his nipples, biting and suckling until he groaned.

"Let's get you out of this little nothing of a frock." His gaze never left hers as he tugged at her shift. The knuckles of his bare hands brushed the small of her back. Shivers and chills ran up and down her spine.

Her nightgown fell to the ground, and he stared at her the way he had that first night, when he'd wrapped her in the stadium blanket. "You are stunning, Elle."

He scooped her up in his arms, and made it as far as a nearby tree. "I'm going to pleasure you, and take pleasure from you." Using the trunk to steady her back, he unzipped his jeans.

She slipped her hand in. Velvet to the touch and throbbing hard, every pure-blooded inch of him vital and potent. She stroked gently at first, teasing him with a light touch. Beneath her fingers, he answered quietly with a twitch.

Half-lidded eyes gleamed in the dark. "Use your claws." No polite request in his gravelly voice, his command was pure need.

Her longer, sharper nails raked over his impressive erection.

He growled softly, and cupped her breasts, massaging their fullness as if he understood the ache inside her. "Closer, love." She arched up and his mouth closed over a nipple, sucking and tugging at the sensitive flesh.

"Abby," she moaned, "I want to see you, feel your body."

He angled back, his gaze riveted on the rosy-beige tip as it ruched into a hard bud. "Beautiful." Fully dilated eyes, nearly devoid of color, perused her body.

Her belly trembled as his inspection moved lower.

"And you are gorgeous," she said, "but I want to see more of you." She was bare-bottom naked, while he remained fully clothed. Hot and sexy to be sure, but she wanted more.

Standing there, with his shirt open and his jeans hanging low on his hips, he took her breath away. Her gaze followed a delicious curve of groin muscle until it vanished beneath his waistband.

She tossed her hair back and thrust her hips at him.

"So impatient," he scolded with a wink. He removed his long coat and spread it over the smooth surface of knoll nearby.

Completely comfortable in his skin, he disrobed in front of her. Muscled chest and abs, but not overly so. Her gaze ravaged his torso. Strong, v-shaped back and gorgeous bum, lean and beautifully sculpted. Having never seen so much of his flesh exposed, she marveled at the cut of his arm muscles, along with a surprise—a beautifully inked, Celtic knot curled around a chiseled bicep.

"A handsome design, for a handsome man."

"The Pendragon knot—de rigueur in our clan." He stowed their clothes beneath an outcropping of rock.

She tore her eyes off the intricate tattoo to admire his long sinewy legs—and oh my—that breathtaking erection.

Abelseth Durant was an insane turn-on.

Humming quietly, her hips swayed to an imaginary rhythm. Long, wavy locks of hair moved with her, concealing then revealing her breasts as she practiced a few dance steps.

"What luck to run across a beautiful naked wood nymph in the forest." He moved up behind her and she reached back and grabbed his ass. Once again, reality shifted, and they were in and out of the drift.

She lay on top of him. "Want to mate?" she teased.

"The most pleasant way to shift is during orgasm," he whispered her ear. "Turn over and rub that cute booty against me."

She rolled over and arched across his torso. "You make for a hard pillow."

"I'll make you'll forget all of that." His husky voice promised, as he coaxed her further into surrender. Never in her life had she felt so open to any man. She raised her arms over her head and stretched out over his body like a human canvas.

Splayed fingers moved over her rib cage, cupping her breasts, teasing taut nipples into harder points.

All she could do was ooh and ahh, and arch her back. Her hips thrust upward and bucked, inviting his hands to slip below her belly.

"Promise me you will be ungentlemanly," she gasped.

"All wolf," he growled softly. "Open wider, love." He dipping a finger in. Circling, rubbing, exploring all the places that made her sigh and go "Ahhh... yes...and oh, Abby..."

Elle had become increasingly aware of a tingling inside, more of an urge than an itch. And there was also a burning sensation, as desire pushed her into wilder territory.

"Once I'm inside you, there will be new sensations as you begin the shift." His fingers stroked the parts of her that wanted more.

Lighter, then harder. Slower, then faster.

Arousal coursed through her body. "You bring me

such pleasure, how could there possibly be more?"

"Oh, my love…" His wet fingers delved deeper. "We have a universe inside us to explore." He used an index finger to tease silken flesh. Edging closer to pure, primal lust, her wolf opened wider. "More," she whispered.

"The change will come at the peak of your pleasure." He nuzzled her neck, and responded with hushed growls and soft kisses. "Your flesh grows supple, I can feel her stretching inside you."

He shifted them both into the drift, turning her in his arms, until he was on top—pressing his knee between her legs. "Kiss me, Elle." She covered his mouth with hers. "More tongue," he demanded and received.

He guided his throbbing erection over folds, sopping wet with her arousal. He held her against him as he filled her with his penis. First a single plunge then another. Each time, he penetrated deeper, until he'd planted himself to the hilt.

His guttural groans joined her breathless gasps. He held her against him, gradually increasing the speed of his thrusts.

"Don't stop," she cried.

"Come for me," he whispered, and she answered him with a snarl. He grabbed hold of her hair and yanked. *A warning to the wolf, love.*

A bolt of orgasm shot through her. "Ah-h, yes, Abby."

He slid his tongue up the side of her neck and took her earlobe in his teeth. "Let go—all the way, Elle."

His cock rubbed slick places that sparked and

quaked and shivered to life. The combination of his rapid thrusts and his finger on her clitoris sent waves of pleasure crashing through her. She cried out in release, then screamed bloody murder as his wolf claws slashed across her hip.

Seconds of sharp, searing pain.

Vaguely, she was aware of his howl.

Her body shuddered from a terrifying mix of pleasure and physical agony. She felt as though she was turning inside out. Every nanoparticle reorganized in seconds—bones, organs, teeth, skin, body hair.

Shooting stars and blackness.

Silence, then awareness.

Gradually, the dark gave way to extraordinary vision. She rose up on four legs, and retreated to one side of the clearing. She could see him clearly—covered in a beautiful coat of fur. He shook himself head to tail, and settled back on his haunches.

Horrified by his ferocious behavior, she licked her wounds, and stared at the wolf that was once Abelseth.

Steady, Elle.

Her muzzle drew back over long white fangs and she growled. *You made me bleed.*

The pain will diminish quickly. What is important is that you are marked. You are safe, now.

She crept closer on four legs. *We are mated, then?*

We are.

She tilted her head. He was a handsome wolf. Gray and white, with lovely shades of biscuit and black markings around his silver eyes.

The sight of your handsome face and coat makes me feel like frolicking.

He lowered his head. *Shall we do some frolicking together?* He approached cautiously, then hesitated.

She dipped her snout, slunk forward, then shied away.

He jumped and dipped around her playfully, provoking a dance of advance and retreat.

Back and forth.

Sniff and snort.

Yip and yelp.

He nuzzled her nose, and the back of her ears. Tentatively, she licked his face and allowed him to rub her—first muzzle to muzzle, then all over.

And she rubbed back, cavorting with him, rolling over, letting him tussle her and explore, before she snarled and snapped at him.

Wolves laughed, at least lycanthrope wolves did. She heard him quite plainly as she ran off into the woods.

Catch me if you can, Abelseth!

EPILOGUE

Happily ever after is really just another beginning.

He found her by the river, wearing nothing but the morning mist, her lithe figure haloed in sunlight. She tossed unruly locks of hair over her shoulder, the wolf in her still so fresh she was hardly aware of her humanness, or her nakedness.

The pretty wood nymph dipped her toe in the water. Captivated, he watched her splash at the inlet's edge. Glistening drops fell over her breasts, hardening tips, dribbling over curves, arousing him beyond all reason.

He ventured closer. "You didn't run away."

She looked up and smiled. "You would have caught me anyway, dragged me back to your den, showered me with amazing orgasms."

He gathered her nightgown in his hand and slipped it over her.

The surface of the Avon rippled with silver and shadings of pale rose. Weir House stood stalwartly at the edge of the forest, keeping watch over the river as it had for hundreds of years.

"A fairy-tale tower—exactly as I remember it." Elle shivered, as much from her recent shift as the chill in the air. He opened his coat, and the dear girl stepped into his arms. "You are a beautiful she-wolf." He cocooned her in warmth, nuzzling her hair, inhaling her scent.

She leaned back, twisting her wild locks and looping them into a casual ponytail. "And you are gray and silver with lovely markings around the eyes and snout—a handsome wolf, indeed."

Elle's peaches and cream complexion glowed. Her wolf was clearly having a positive effect on her. "It's odd to meet another side of yourself. She's familiar and yet she's completely new." A wide smile crinkled her pretty eyes. "Is it rude to speak about my wolf in third person?"

He grinned. "In some ways, females take to shifting with greater ease than males." Elle continually astounded him. Her first shift had been near effortless, and she had shown a good deal of agility and cunning. In their run through the woods, they'd twice encountered other wolves, all of them servile and respectful. She'd quickly understood their function both as pack members and four-legged guards of their alpha's mate.

She'd even allowed them to greet her, quite intimately, as wolves often do. On the downside, their attentions had stimulated an alpha display the likes of which his pack had never witnessed.

"You can be quite ferocious in your wolf form." She hugged him tight and kissed him.

"It's a show of dominance, to warn them off you. He nudged her nose with his. "It wasn't meant to frighten you."

"I wasn't frightened." A pale shade of rose warmed

her cheeks. "I was excited—aroused, maybe?"

"And you survived your first shift with flying colors." He drew her closer. "I'm afraid I came along and interrupted your wolf avoidance plans."

"Upended them," she exhaled a sigh. A stray lock of hair fell across her eye. "And I've gone and complicated your bachelor wolf status."

"You've made a complete bollix out of it." He swept the errant hair behind her ear. "How quickly life can change. Suddenly, I have someone to care for."

He straightened to view more of her. "I do hope I'm forgiven for those ghastly red gashes." She stepped away and he raised the hem of her shift, enough to reveal his mark.

A slash of claws swept over the curve of her hip, primitive and possessive. "They'll look fierce in a bikini," he murmured.

Her eyes sparkled with light. "Might we go on a holiday? Someplace beachy—I must show them off." She rolled her hip and gave her bottom a playful slap.

"I shall book leave and take my beautiful wife on a proper honeymoon." He reached out. "Come, I'll scramble some eggs for us."

She took his hand. "Warning—I toast crumpets for breakfast."

"Then I will scramble, and you will toast."

They started down the gentle slope toward Weir House. "I'll not be one of those trophy wives adorning your arm, wearing a tight black sheath, chatting up people I hardly know at cocktail parties."

"Yes to the tight black sheath, no to everything

else."

Her bottom lip protruded slightly. "And I'll not be darning socks or baking pies."

"I'm used to buying new socks and I can bring home pies."

"Listen to us." She sighed. "We're bickering again."

Laughing softly, he answered her with a wink and a nod.

~ The End ~

About Jillian . . .

Jillian Stone is the author of the Phaeton Black, Paranormal Detective series, which includes *The Seduction of Phaeton Black, The Moonstone and Miss Jones,* and *The Miss Education of Dr. Exeter.*

Can't get enough of British detectives? Jillian has also written the Gentlemen of Scotland Yard Romantic Suspense series, which includes, *An Affair With Mr. Kennedy, A Dangerous Liaison with Detective Lewis, A Private Duel with Agent Gunn,* and *A Lesson in Chemistry with Inspector Bruce.*

Looking for something edgy and different? Try Jillian's recent release, *Eat, Slay, Luzt,* a sexy wild ride into the dark heart of the zombie apocalypse. Or if you're in the mood for something sizzling-hot and contemporary there's *The Do It List.*

All of Jillian's books are available in digital and print formats from on-line retailers.

Find out more at Jillian's web site:
www.jillianstone.com
And be sure to visit Jillian on Facebook:
JillianStoneBooks

www.ingramcontent.com/pod-product-compliance
Lightning Source LLC
Chambersburg PA
CBHW021225130626
46554CB00004B/1375